Ben tugged her zipper open with his teeth

Taylor thought she had died and gone to heaven. It was unbelievably erotic to have him on the floor in front of her, knowing he could touch her anywhere, do anything. He kissed her right below her belly button, and she whimpered in pure surrender.

"Oh, God," he whispered, just before he licked the expanse of flesh above her lace panties.

Oh, no. The thought of where he was going, what he was going to lick next, made her hot. She wanted him to hurry, to rip off the rest of her clothes and throw her on the bed.

Restlessly she put her hands on his head and ran her fingers through his dark hair. "Stand up, please."

Ben looked up and smiled. "Are you sure?" At her nod, he got up from his knees, kissed her hard. Let his body lean against her and she felt his erection through his soft jeans.

He gazed at her. "Why did we wait so long?"

She laughed. "We just got here last night."

"Ten years," he said. "I missed too much."

Her hand went to his face where she traced his lips. "I'm here now. And we definitely need to make up for lost time…."

Blaze™

Dear Reader,

Oh, what a special book this is to me! The story, while fictional, is based in part on something that happened to me....

Twenty-five years ago (argh!) I met the man of my dreams. He was everything I ever wanted in a guy. Only, the romance ended after a few years. Ended badly. But I never did get over him. He was The One Who Got Away, and it took me a long time to make peace with the fact that I'd never meet a man who could compare.

Flash forward twenty years, and bless the Internet. Because guess who found me? You got it. The One! We talked, and talked...and three months later, we moved in together. He's no longer the one who got away, but he's still The One!

So that's how Taylor and Ben came about. Although the details are different, the incredible gift of finding (and keeping!) a lost love are just the same.

Affectionately yours,

Jo Leigh

Books by Jo Leigh

HARLEQUIN BLAZE

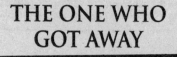

THE ONE WHO GOT AWAY

Jo Leigh

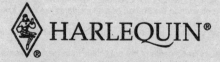

HARLEQUIN®

TORONTO • NEW YORK • LONDON
AMSTERDAM • PARIS • SYDNEY • HAMBURG
STOCKHOLM • ATHENS • TOKYO • MILAN • MADRID
PRAGUE • WARSAW • BUDAPEST • AUCKLAND

To Lawrence: The One Who (Almost) Got Away!

ISBN 0-373-79138-0

THE ONE WHO GOT AWAY

Copyright © 2004 by Jolie Kramer.

Prologue

To: The Gang at Eve's Apple
From Taylor
EvesApple.com
Subject: BEN!!!!!

If you're looking for something soft, you won't find it in Ben's face. Not at first.

He is all hard lines and sharp angles. The cheekbones, of course. The stuff of dreams. Improbable. Dangerous. Unforgettable. The cheekbones make you look at his eyes, give you no choice. They're dark and knowing. Too knowing. Which makes you look away, but not for long. The focus shifts to his lips. The upper is thin, but there. The pouty lower makes up for it. And when the corners of his lips curve up in that slight smile, when those eyes take you in from the toes up, when he flicks his dark, straight, too-long hair back with a hand, there's nothing to do but surrender. Give it up. Lie down, whether you're near a bed or not.

That's Ben. My first lover. My best lover. Might as well have been my only lover. Because it's been ten years, and I can't get that face out of my head.

Every man I've dated, from that gorgeous Richard

Gere-like attorney to that race-car driver from Atlanta has failed the Ben Test. Not that I even realized there was such a thing, but now that I know I'm going to see Ben again, I finally get it. I see what he's done to me.

So, my fellow Eve's Apple Compatriots, my sisters in righteous conquests who seek the perfect Men To Do before we say I Do...I hereby declare that Ben Bowman, the man of the exquisite cheekbones, of the mesmerizing dark eyes, is my official MAN TO DO.

I, Taylor Hanson, am going to spend one week with the aforementioned Mr. Bowman, in, appropriately enough, Las Vegas, Sin City, while attending my brother's wedding. I will, without fail, get Ben "Cheekbones" Bowman into my bed, and then I will see, with my very own eyes, that regardless of cheekbones, of knowing eyes, and wicked smiles, Bowman is just a guy. Like a bunch of other guys. Not a God, not an icon, not the King of the Stud Muffins.

I was only eighteen.

And then, my dear friends, I will come home, and I SHALL BE FREE to find my Mr. Right. My forever guy. Because I will have broken the spell. Damn it.

Love and Kisses,

Taylor

1

ONLY IN VEGAS.

Ben watched the crowd standing in front of the Wheel of Fortune slot machine as he made his way through the airline terminal toward the baggage claim area. Breathless with anticipation, a dozen or so tourists watched the spinning wheel as it slowed, coming to a shaky stop under the bold 20. A collective groan marked their disappointment, and Ben marveled again at the gullibility of humans.

All anyone needed to do was take one look at the Strip to see that Vegas wasn't in the business of giving away money. But most of the good folk who came to Vegas didn't stop to think about the odds. They came for magic. For the turn of the wheel, the flip of a card that would free them from the daily grind of working for a living. They wanted the dream and no place on earth knew how to sell the dream better.

Not that Ben didn't mind a friendly game of poker now and then, but he had no illusions about windfalls or magic. He believed in hard work and persistence. If luck ever entered the picture it was because he'd made sure to be in the right place at the right time.

He passed the shops selling overpriced leather jackets, gaudy trinkets and T-shirts, finally arriving at the escalator that would take him down to his the baggage claim area.

As was his wont, he'd checked in at the last possible moment, assuring that his luggage would be some of the first out of the plane. In fact, this time his bag was the very first. A few minutes later, he was in a cab on his way to the Hard Rock Hotel.

He stared at the vision that was Las Vegas as the cab made its way along Paradise Road. How appropriate. The Hard Rock wasn't on the Strip per se, but two blocks east. Still it managed to be the hippest of the big hotels. He'd never stayed there, but he'd had dinner at Nobu and the Pink Taco. Nice place, if you liked that sort of thing. He didn't. Give him a mountain lake and a fishing pole, and he was all set. Glitz and glamour made him itchy, but this was Steve's wedding, and he'd have gone to the far side of the moon for that.

It puzzled him, however. Steve Hanson had been his closest friend since the fifth grade, and while they hadn't lived in the same town since college, they still got together twice a year to go deep-sea fishing. It made things easier that Steve owned the boats. Five of them, actually, all moored in his and Steve's hometown, San Diego. Steve had eschewed the white-collar life of his father to follow the beat of his own drum. He'd started out with one boat, *The Golden Mermaid,* and had increased his fleet by a boat every other year for ten years. He'd made himself a good life, and as far as Ben could see, he was a truly happy man. What Ben couldn't see was why he was about to change all that.

He hadn't discussed his plans with Ben, or the reasons behind his decision. There had just been that one phone call where Steve had asked him to come to Vegas, to be his best man. He'd said his fiancée's name was Lisa, and that she was the best thing that had ever happened to him. He'd also said that he was going to keep the fleet but move to Kansas, and work for her father at his aerospace company. That was the kicker. The puzzle. Steve hated corporate life, had broken his father's heart by not taking over the family insurance business. So why now? Why her? Why marriage?

The cab turned into the big driveway, underneath the huge guitar that was the Hard Rock logo. The lot was crowded with every kind of vehicle from Hummers to limos to beat-up Chevys. At the entrance, a uniformed doorman tried to help but Ben took his suitcase to the front desk. His room, on the fourteenth floor, was ready and after a long walk through the noisy casino, and another down a silent padded hallway, he reached it.

The parlor of his deluxe room had gold walls, green carpeting, a semicircular couch with a round black coffee table, a wet bar and, behind purple drapes that framed French doors, a fabulous view of the Strip. The bedroom wasn't quite as fancy, but nice. Two queen platform beds with leather headboards, a built-in TV instead of the usual armoire and another spectacular view.

He tossed his suitcase onto the bed, then noticed the light on his phone blinking. He punched the numbers to get the message. It was Steve, sounding chip-

per, asking him to dinner. They were to meet at the
front desk in about three hours, long enough for Ben
to have a shower and a nap. The last part of the message was that Taylor would be joining the party, and
that she was looking forward to seeing him.

Taylor.

Ben hung up the phone, but he didn't move. She'd
been a little kid when he'd first met her: Steve's baby
sister. She'd followed them wherever she could, always wanting attention, always wanting to be let in
on the fun. They'd ditched her as often a possible,
and he could still remember her tears.

But mostly he remembered the last time he'd seen
her. It had to be ten years ago, just after she'd graduated from high school. He'd been at his folk's house
for their thirtieth wedding anniversary, and had stayed
on for a week while they'd gone on the second honeymoon cruise to the Virgin Islands he'd treated them
to. Taylor had come by on a Friday afternoon and
she'd stayed until Sunday.

She'd grown into a beauty and when she'd come
on to him, he hadn't the will or the strength to turn
her away.

The weekend had been one of the most exciting of
his life. She'd been a wildcat, and he'd loved every
second of it. She'd cried when he'd said goodbye, but
he'd known the tears were more about the end of a
fantasy than any real heartbreak.

Taylor had been heading off for college, for a
whole new life that had nothing to do with childhood
crushes. He'd returned to the New York police force,
determined to become a sergeant. By the time he'd

settled back into his regular routine, he'd felt certain she'd forgotten all about him.

It would be good to see her again. According to Steve, she'd never married. Smart girl.

Ben glanced at the clock, and got up. He didn't want to be late for dinner.

TAYLOR CHECKED herself out one last time before she had to leave. Her hair wasn't too horrifying, although she would have to buy some kind of conditioner that would give it some lift. She'd put on her makeup with care, and felt she'd hit the right combination of come-hither and stay there. After trying on every item of clothing she'd brought, she'd ended up wearing a cute little Michael Kors she'd picked up at a ritzy second-hand store. It was black, sleeveless, and skintight, with kicky leather shoulders that made her boobs look much bigger than they were. She'd have to hold in her stomach the entire night, but it was worth it. She wanted Ben's jaw to drop the moment he saw her. She sucked in harder. Realizing that she couldn't go the entire night without a breath, she gave it up.

So she pooched. He probably had love handles.

She got her purse, made sure she had her room key, and headed off to the elevator, her pulse racing faster with each step.

By the time she reached the casino level, she was practically hyperventilating. What had she been thinking? She hadn't seen the man in ten years, she had no idea what his life was like. For all she knew, he could have brought a lover with him. Steve hadn't mentioned anything about Ben being attached, but then Steve was a notoriously bad gossip. He'd had all kinds of famous people on his boats, and had he ever brought home one juicy tidbit? Never. She hated that.

And she hated the butterflies in her stomach. This wasn't going to work. Taylor leaned against a large display case exhibiting stage clothes worn by Shania Twain. The woman had to weigh twelve pounds, the outfit was so tiny. But that was beside the point. Taylor had to do something, and do it now. She could go back to her room, call Steven and say she didn't feel well, but that would only delay the inevitable. She couldn't stay in her room the whole week. What made oodles more sense was for her to forget about her Man To Do plan and just go enjoy her brother's happiness. Forget about Ben and his cheekbones. If he looked anything like he had, there was no way he would be single. No woman could possibly resist him, and living in New York, he was up to his deliciously square chin in stunning babes.

She straightened her shoulders, flicked her hair back and pasted on a smile. Tonight, in fact this whole week, wasn't about her. It was about her brother. For heaven's sake, she hadn't even met Lisa yet, and she was going to be her sister-in-law. With that thought firmly in mind, she once again headed toward the lobby, letting the sounds of bells, coins, music and chatter ease her way.

So what if she didn't get her Man To Do? She had her vibrator, and that was a relationship she could count on.

BEN SPOTTED STEVE standing near the Jimi Hendrix display. He had his arm around a tall, slim blonde.

She was frowning, but even so, she was pretty. A different kind of pretty for Steve. The women he went for tended to look like Playboy Bunnies. They partied like Bunnies, too. But Ben didn't get that feeling from Lisa. She was dressed in white slacks, a pale blue top and a white jacket, tailored, classy; more Midwest than So Cal. Her hair was neat, not quite to her shoulders, and her shoes and purse were both white and conservative. She looked like she'd be right at home in a country club or on a golf course, not on one of Steve's boats.

Ben kept on walking, shaking off his first impressions. One thing he'd learned the hard way was that looks don't mean squat. He'd judge Lisa for who she was behind the Ralph Lauren look.

Steve turned, and grinned like he'd just caught a two-hundred pound swordfish. "Ben, you old bastard!"

Ben shook his head. Some things didn't change, thank God. "I didn't know they let people like you in here. Where's security?"

Steve let go of his girl and gave Ben a rib bruising hug. "Thanks for coming, man."

"Oh, right. Like I'd let you get married without me? Someone's got to tell her what she's getting into."

Steve laughed, that big hearty guffaw that was as distinct as his fingerprints. It made Ben feel like he was home.

"This—" Steve said, moving toward his lady "—is Lisa."

Ben met her gaze, liked her smile. Close up, she was attractive, but subtly so. Her blue eyes seemed a little hesitant, judging him. Which was only fair, he supposed. "Nice to meet you, Lisa."

"Steven has told me so much about you."

"Uh-oh. Remember, innocent until proven guilty."

She laughed, then took Steve's arm. "Do you think we should call your sister? I don't want to lose our reservation."

"Let's give her another— Wait. There she is."

Ben turned to follow Steve's gaze. He wasn't in the least prepared for what he was about to see.

TAYLOR SLOWED as she got her first look at Ben Bowman. *Oh, shit.* He'd changed, all right. He'd become the most devastatingly handsome man she'd ever laid eyes on.

Her legs wobbled beneath her, but she focused on putting one foot in front of the other, and not falling on her fanny. She didn't know what to look at first. No, not true, the cheekbones were first, they had to be, and holy mama, they were even more chiseled than she remembered. His eyes seemed darker, but she'd need to be closer to be sure. He still wore his hair long, just past his ears. It wasn't neat or tidy in the least. It didn't need to be. He looked like he'd just gotten out of bed. And she meant that in the best possible way.

Her fingers twitched, itching to run through those dark locks, to see those familiar lips curl up in a wicked smile.

Okay, so she was back to the original plan. Sleep

with him or die trying. She could do it. She had to do it. Hell, there was a long couch just this side of the lobby that looked pretty comfortable.

Finally, seconds before she was close enough to actually speak to Ben, her gaze shifted down. His body was every bit as wonderful as her memory had promised. Not the tallest guy on the block, but perfectly proportioned. He wore jeans, well-worn, cowboy boots beneath them. His shirt was white, no tie, his jacket hunter green. Altogether a delicious package.

No way he wasn't taken. Not possible.

"Taylor, hello?"

Startled, she looked at her brother. "Hi."

Steve laughed, shook his head. "I see you remember Ben."

Heat filled her cheeks as she forced herself to forget about Ben and concentrate on her brother and his wife-to-be. After a quick kiss and a poke to his shoulder, she said, "Well? Are you going to introduce me?"

Steve stepped over to the woman in the white pantsuit and put his arm around her shoulders. "Taylor, this is Lisa. The woman who's changed my whole life."

Taylor smiled and moved in for an awkward air kiss. To say she was surprised was an understatement. *This* was Lisa? This preppy sorority sister? Not possible. Taylor glanced at Ben, and from his practiced look, she could tell she wasn't the only one who thought something was screwy here.

But she wasn't being fair. She hadn't even talked

to Lisa, so maybe inside those Alpha-Gamma-Delta clothes there lived the soul of a wild woman.

"Everybody hungry?"

Taylor turned to Steve. "Starving. Where are we eating?"

"I thought we'd go over to the Venetian tonight. Eat at The Grand Luxe."

"Great."

He turned to Lisa, his gaze adoring. "I'll go get a cab," he said.

"I'll come with you. Give Taylor and Ben a chance to catch up."

They walked away, leaving her alone with *him* and awkwardness swallowed her whole. She smiled, turned toward the big glass doors with the guitar-shaped pulls.

"It's been a while," Ben said, moving closer to her, ratcheting up the heat in the casino by a good ten degrees. "You look great."

"Thanks. So do you."

His low chuckle made her look. The moment their eyes met, she was lost—eighteen again, fumbling, frightened, drowning in lust.

Ben watched as Taylor's eyes dilated, the pale blue shrinking to a thin halo. Her lips parted, revealing the tops of her even, white teeth. Her cheeks turned from pastel pink to dark, and he thought of her breasts, remembering clearly the shape of her nipples, the color of her areoles matching exactly her blush.

He let his gaze wander to her lips: plump, glisten-ing, inviting, then down her remarkable neck, long and elegant, like Audrey Hepburn's, only Taylor was blond, a real blonde, with long straight hair that flowed down her back, that rippled in the artificial lights of the lobby. Her figure had changed, all for the better. At eighteen, she'd been so slender he'd been afraid of hurting her. Now, her hips had become womanly, her breasts a perfect handful. But she still had the silky skin of a teenager.

That weekend so long ago had rocked his world. Had made him realize what making love could be. Had taken him from fair-to-middling to a pretty damn skilled lover. He'd remembered it from time to time, always with a smile. But he'd never once thought there could be a repeat. Time and life had a way of softening the edges of memories. He had no desire to refocus, to see the inevitable chinks and flaws that ride along with reality.

Oh, who was he kidding. He'd beg if he had to.

2

"WE'D BETTER get out there," Taylor said. "They probably have the cab ready."

"Right." Ben waited until she started walking toward the front entrance to move next to her, to place his hand at the small of her back. He felt her shiver as he touched her.

She cleared her throat. "So you're living in New York."

"Yep. Manhattan."

"I love that city. Where?"

"What used to be called Hell's Kitchen. Now it's almost as trendy as Tribeca."

"You must hate that."

"I do. But there's nothing to be done. I've got my office in the same building, two stories down. I don't want to move."

"What's it like being a private eye?"

"It's just like in the movies. Smoky bars, jazz playing in the background, fallen women, men with dark pasts and unregistered guns."

"Cute," she said, as they got outside.

The heat shocked him again, like when he'd come from the airport. Not that it wasn't hot in Manhattan, but here it didn't stick to your skin like wet towels.

Taylor must have noticed his reaction. "It was in the low seventies when I left this morning," she said. "Oh, there they are."

Steve was standing beside a Yellow Cab. "You're in San Francisco, right?"

She nodded. "Right near Lombardi. The apartment is too expensive, but I love riding my bike there."

"Ten speed?"

"Honda Shadow."

He stopped short. A motorcycle? Interesting. "You'll have to tell me all about it."

Before she slid into the cab, she smiled at him. "Oh, I plan to."

He watched her maneuver onto the back seat, which was quite a feat considering the tightness of her dress. She did well, very much the lady. But he had a feeling that was only for show. At least he hoped so.

Steve got in beside her, and Ben got in front. The ride to the Venetian wasn't long. It would have been shorter, but for the masses of tourists. Still, it was better than trying to get through Manhattan on a busy evening.

He'd never been to the Venetian, and was impressed with the high arched ceilings and the frescos on the walls. Even the floor tiles were European and stately, somehow managing to appear subdued and classy. After a long walk past a lot of high-end shops, through the casino, they arrived at the café.

Steve ushered them inside, past a considerable line, into the large, beautifully decorated restaurant. It also had decked-out ceilings, fancy floors and great leather booths. The bar looked as if it served expensive martinis, but the crowd seemed happy and from what he could see on the plates held aloft by the waitstaff, no one would leave hungry.

A waitress showed them to their booth, and he slid in next to Taylor. It was roomy, which wasn't necessarily a good thing when one was sitting beside a woman in a tiny dress. But he wasn't going to go there. Not yet, at least. Tonight was for Steve.

The happy couple kissed after they got their menus. Steve smiled broadly, Lisa more conservatively, but that didn't mean anything. She opened her menu and studied it carefully, her brows furrowing slightly as if the choice was crucial.

Ben glanced down, only it would take more than a glance to get through the choices in the book they called a menu. He decided on something he could always trust, a New York Sirloin steak and baked potato.

Their waitress took their drink orders, and then it was just the four of them.

"All right," Taylor said, putting her menu aside. "I want to hear it all. Omit nothing. How you met, when you fell in love, why you decided to get married in Vegas, the whole nine yards."

Steve laughed and Lisa gave a tentative grin. But then Lisa was the stranger amongst them, and that had to be hard.

Ben liked Taylor's style. Come right out with it. No beating around the bush. She'd always been like that, since the time she was a little kid, demanding to play touch football when she could hardly hold the ball. The only time she'd been reticent had been that last weekend, but he figured it was the newness of the situation. He imagined that had changed.

"We met on the *Turquoise Mermaid*," Steve said. "Her dad was fishing and Lisa decided to join him and his buddies for the day. She didn't fish, which turned out to be a good thing because we started talking and just kept right on going."

"I hadn't even wanted to go," Lisa said, leaning in to the table, her eyes brighter now that they were on a subject she could dive into. "But my father insisted, although he was with Trent Foster and Cal Peterson. Cal brought his wife, Annie, who is closer to my age than his, so Daddy dragged me along. But Annie got horribly seasick, and she didn't want to talk to anyone, which left me free to concentrate on the wildly handsome skipper."

Steve's grin widened. "I got so involved with Lisa it almost cost her father a swordfish. But we nailed him." He leaned over and kissed her cheek. "Didn't we?"

"We? I got as far away as I could. I had no idea swordfish were so big and so dangerous." She settled back in the booth. "At least we won't have to worry about that anymore."

Taylor didn't like the sound of that. "What do you mean?"

"She means I'm letting Larry take over the management of the fleet," Steve said. "Once we're married, I'm moving to Kansas. Her dad's offered me a hell of a good job in sales and marketing. I don't know much about the aerospace industry yet, but I'm learning. They make seals, connectors, gaskets, that kind of thing. Real high-end stuff, the highest temperature seals in the industry. I'll be traveling a lot. Except for missing Lisa, I think it'll be great. I mean, they have this major air show in France every year. Of course, she'll come with me.''

Taylor was grateful the waitress arrived with their drinks so she had a moment to absorb what she'd just heard. Her brother hated working in an office. He'd built his life around the freedom of the sea. This was a complete one-eighty, and it made her nervous as hell. She sipped her Cosmopolitan, glanced at Ben, whose expression mirrored her own concern. ''So Larry's going to run the fleet, huh? You're okay with that?''

Steve's grin faltered. ''Yeah, sure. He'll do a great job. He's been with me for six years now, and he knows everything about the job.''

''But Kansas?'' Taylor leaned in, trying like hell to make Steve look her in the eyes. ''No sailing? No fishing? It's what you love best in all the world.''

''He won't miss it,'' Lisa said. ''And we'll visit San Diego often enough for him to keep his sea legs. You know how bright he is, though, and it's a shame to waste that on fishing. He has a brilliant career in front of him. I'm sure one day he'll take over the company. My father always wanted a son, and now he'll have one.''

''You had no interest in the business?'' Ben asked.

Lisa laughed. ''God, no. I have my own interior design firm. I've done some of the largest homes in Wichita.''

"Really?" Taylor said, her concern deepening by the second.

"Oh, yes. I absolutely love it. My mother works with me, and we have a wonderful assistant, Renee. Right now I work out of mother's house, but when Steve and I build our home, we'll include an office. That way, when we have children, I'll be able to be nearby all the time."

"Wow. It sounds like you've got the whole thing worked out."

"We do," Steve said. "Like Lisa says, it's time for me to grow up. Take on the real world. I can't be Peter Pan forever." He kissed her again, lightly on the cheek.

The waitress came back to take their dinner orders. Taylor stole another look at Ben, and he wasn't disguising his worry in the least. Lisa seemed like a very nice woman and all, but this was nuts. Steve would be miserable working in sales. He hated that kind of thing, and without an ocean nearby, he'd go stir-crazy.

"It seems like all this happened pretty damn fast," Ben said.

"It all just fell into place," Steve said. He held on to his drink with both hands. "I'd been thinking a lot about my life, what I was doing with it. Sure, it's fun helping a bunch of rich guys catch trophy fish, but, I don't know…"

"My father took to him from the moment they met." Lisa smiled. "Just like I did. He saw the potential in Steve. He's a brilliant salesman. There's no reason on earth he can't use those talents in the real world. He could take Daddy's business to the top.''

''It sounds lucrative.''

''Oh, yeah.'' Steve nodded. ''I'll be making more than I ever dreamed of.''

''I didn't know you dreamed about money.'' Taylor wished she could say more, remind him of how he'd laughed at all those poor schmucks chasing a dime. But it wasn't the time or the place. She needed to think. If this truly was the direction Steve wanted to go, then who was she to butt in? Although it felt wrong. Seriously wrong.

''Of course I think about money. Who doesn't? I mean, if it was just me, it wouldn't matter. But with a wife and kids... How could I put the time into the boats? You know the life. Living at the pier, away for days at a time, no regular schedules.''

''I suppose so,'' she said.

Ben lifted his glass. ''To new roads.''

She joined in the toast, all the while feeling like her brother wasn't heading down a new road, but off a cliff.

BEN HELD THE TAXI DOOR for Taylor, unable to look away from the expanse of thigh her short dress revealed. Despite his genuine and deep concern for his friend, a large part of him had been preoccupied with the woman at his side. No matter what was happening with his frontal lobe, the primal part of his brain had locked on to Taylor, her scent, the way her hair cascaded down her shoulder, the curve of her breasts.

His plan was to ditch Steve and Lisa, which wasn't

going to be too difficult, as Lisa had already said she was beat, and get Taylor to himself. So they could talk. That's all. Talk about Steve.

Steve paid off the cab, then turned to the small group. "We're going to our room. We have to be up at the crack of dawn to pick up Lisa's mom at the airport."

"When's our mom coming in?" Taylor asked.

"Tomorrow afternoon."

"Do you need me to get her?"

"Nope, we have it covered." Steve kissed his sister on the cheek. "But thanks. Why don't you and Ben go have some fun? Win a little dough."

"Right," she said. "You know how lucky I am with cards."

Steve laughed. "Okay, so don't play poker."

"I still maintain that you cheat every chance you get."

He held his hand up to his chest as if shocked. "Me? Never."

"Yeah, right."

"Thanks for the dinner, you two. We'll catch up with you tomorrow," Ben said.

"Great."

Lisa said good-night, then took Steve's hand. Taylor watched them walk into the hotel. Ben watched Taylor.

"This is weird as hell," he said, as soon as they'd entered the lobby.

"I'll say. Did you have any idea?"

He shook his head. "Last I heard, he was thinking about buying another boat."

"He asked me to quit my damn boring job and come work for him. He said I was a fool for wasting my life," Taylor added.

"So what changed?"

Taylor shook her head. "Love?"

"I don't know…"

Ben wanted to touch her again, as he had on the way out. Gently, palm to the small of her back. He wanted to feel her quiver. Instead, he put his hands in his pockets.

"I want to talk to Mom about it," Taylor said. "Maybe she knows."

"Good idea." He stopped just before they reached the main casino floor. "Are you too tired for a drink? We could go outside by the pool."

She smiled and he thought he detected a slight blush. "That sounds great."

"Good." He took her hand, which might have been better than touching her back, and led her through the youngish crowd. Everyone was on the right side of dressy, trying to look hip. The music, loud enough to make people shout to be heard, was only the coolest rock. Right now they were playing Stevie Ray Vaughn from his second album. Although there were lots of people playing video poker and slots, they were mostly silent, concentrating on whatever voodoo they had to mesmerize the machines. The real hubbub came from the craps tables.

Ben and Taylor threaded through the winners and losers until they got to a hall leading past a couple of high-end restaurants, to the door to the pool. A guard stood at the exit, and they had to show their room keys.

After that, they stepped into a lush, green paradise. The pool area, one of the prettiest in Vegas, had a lot of night swimmers gliding about, mostly by the swim-up bar and the water blackjack tables. But that's not where Ben wanted to be. He led Taylor past the purple lounge chairs and the swaying palms 'til they passed the huge bar. Once there, they climbed a few steps to reach the cabana level. He hoped he'd find one empty, and luck was with him. During the day, the cabanas could be rented for a bundle, but after ten, if you were lucky, you could homestead. The refuse from another party still cluttered the small round table, but that wasn't a problem.

He ushered Taylor to one of the green padded chairs, and he sat next to her. The television in the corner was off, which was what he wanted, and the overhead fan was on, creating a nice breeze in the semiprivate space. He'd like it even better if he could close the curtain, but he didn't want to scare her.

"This is unbelievable," she said. "I haven't been here before, but I'd heard about the cabanas."

"They're not easy to reserve," he said, "although sometimes you can get lucky."

She leaned back in her chair and crossed her legs. It was a sight he wouldn't soon forget. The long stretch of bare thigh, the perfection of her knee, the subtle curve of her calf. To say nothing of the arch of her foot, and the seduction of her high black heel. He felt as mesmerized as a compulsive gambler staring at a royal flush.

It was the waitress that brought him out of his daze. She of the black leather short-shorts, leopard-print vest and perky smile. "What can I get you?"

Taylor ordered a piña colada, he got a scotch on the rocks. The waitress cleared their table, then hustled off, leaving them in the relative quiet. The music, now something by Tom Petty, wafted in along with the laughter and muffled chatter from the group at the bar.

Taylor leaned toward him. "It's good to see you, Ben."

His gaze moved up to her eyes radiating fondness that touched him unexpectedly. "You, too."

"You probably know how horrible Steve is at gossip, so I don't know much of what's happened to you other than you're now a private investigator. Are you happy?"

"For the most part. I like being my own boss."

"That makes sense."

"But I still work with the NYPD a lot. More than I figured."

"Interesting stuff?"

"Occasionally. Mostly it's the kind of footwork that takes a special know-how." He chuckled. "That makes it sound like I'm some Colombo or something. I meant that I do the kind of background checks that don't make it into the NCIC. Paperwork traces, poking into things that might get dicey for the force. That kind of thing."

"I think it sounds fascinating."

"How kind of you."

"I'm more interested in your personal life. Again, according to my brother, you're divorced."

"For two years now."

She ran her hand down her thigh to her knee. Not scratching, just an unconscious gesture that held him rapt. Odd, because it had been a hell of a long time since he'd been spellbound by a woman. Maybe it was the memories. Or the fact that he'd had to get up before God this morning and he was getting punchy.

"I'm sorry," she said. "Was it bad?"

"I can't think of a divorce that isn't. But we're friends. In fact, we still occasionally make a night of it."

Taylor's brows lifted.

"Not that much of a night. Alyson's gay."

Taylor's brows stayed lifted.

"You can imagine how that went over with all my cop buddies."

"Oh, my."

"At the very least. But I don't think I'm too emotionally scarred. I vent my anguish by boycotting all reruns of *Ellen*."

Her laughter hit him low, like a vibration right in the balls. It felt good, too good.

The drinks arrived, and she tried to pay. He used his best scowl, and gave the waitress too large a tip. Once they were alone again, he sipped his scotch, aware that it was either going to make him drunk as a sailor or put him to sleep. "So what are we going to do about this wedding thing?"

Taylor twirled her drink with her straw. It made the

little umbrella spin. "I'm not sure there's anything we can do. Or should."

"Are you kidding? Can you honestly see Steve in a suit and tie, doing aircraft sales in the middle of friggin' Kansas?"

She shook her head. "No, I can't. But maybe he's had some sort of epiphany. Maybe we should honor that."

"Epiphany? Steve? Are we talking about the same guy?"

Her sigh echoed his own frustration. "I know. Let me talk to Mom. I don't want to jump the gun."

"He's getting married in six days."

"Look, the last thing I want to do is hurt him. He's such a puppy. And I know he's lonely."

Ben grinned. "I've never thought of him as a puppy, but I do agree about the lonely part. It's not easy to find a woman who likes to fish as much as he does."

"That doesn't mean he has to go in the opposite direction. I could even understand a compromise. But this…this is nuts."

"I agree."

She sipped again, and he focused on her lips. Glossy-pink. Perfectly formed, ripe for kissing. She'd become an uncommon beauty, and if his signals weren't crossed, she wasn't averse to the idea of making this week quite memorable. However, it wasn't going to be remembered for tonight. The dollop of scotch had gone straight to his head, and if he didn't get up to the room soon, things were going to get ugly.

"Taylor," he said, "I hate to cut the party short, but I'm going to have to bail. I was up way too early this morning."

She put her drink down on the table, and he would swear she looked guilty. Why? He hadn't a clue.

"No problem. I need to get some sleep myself." She stood, smoothing her short skirt down. "Are you going to be around tomorrow? I'll talk to Mom as soon as I can."

He pulled out his wallet, then one of his cards. "Try my room, but if not, I've got my cell."

"Terrific." Her smile made him weak in the knees. He stood, held out his hand. "Can I walk you up?"

"Thank you, but actually, I need to pick up something at the gift shop. You go on ahead."

Disappointed, he nodded. Leaned over and kissed her cheek. Wanted to do a lot more. But he backed off. What he needed was sleep. He wanted to be on his game for Taylor. Nothing less would do. "Until tomorrow."

She nodded, and as he walked away, he heard that sigh again. It almost made him turn around, but he held the course. Although he made his living interpreting nonverbal cues, he couldn't figure this one out. Either she was glad to get rid of him, or damn sorry to see him go.

He chose to believe it was the latter.

3

TAYLOR WATCHED BEN get into the elevator. He smiled at her, not noticing that behind him, a tall brunette in shorts was eyeing him with palpable lust. Or maybe he did know. Maybe he'd grown so accustomed to gorgeous women wanting him that it was old hat by now. The elevator doors closed while she still had her hand up, waving.

She wasn't sure why she'd told him she had to buy something. In fact, she didn't need a thing, and for all she knew the gift shop was closed by now. Instead, she wandered into the circular casino, her gaze shifting from the machines to the gamblers at the tables.

She'd never done much playing herself, even though she'd come to Vegas several times since she'd turned twenty-one. Mostly she liked to hang out at the blackjack tables—the cheap ones, not those with a minimum bet of twenty-five dollars. She wasn't rich enough to squander money like that. And normally, she wasn't an extraordinary risk-taker. Her mother didn't believe that, given her preference for motorcycles over cars, but it was true. There were only so many chances a person could take in life, and she wanted to make her gambles count.

Like her personal agenda for this trip, for example.

Sleeping with Ben wasn't so much a gamble as a last-ditch attempt to get herself back on course. She was twenty-eight, for heaven's sake, and dammit, she wanted to get married. Have kids. Two, to be precise. And she had no intention of settling.

Sure there had been nice guys, and she'd liked one or two a great deal. But it hadn't been enough. Perhaps her friends from Eve's Apple were right: she was too picky. She wanted a fairy-tale hero, not a real-life husband. What Taylor didn't understand was why she had to have one or the other. And no, she didn't feel as if she were reaching for the moon.

The truth was, she liked her life. She didn't sit around and mope because she wasn't married. She had lots of things she loved doing, including her bike, shooting pool in her league, going to flea markets, reading, a secret addiction to the Food Channel. She never felt bored, she always had a full plate, and for the most part, she was happy. All she really wanted was someone to share it all with. And, oh, God, how she wanted to have kids.

The Apple gals had suggested she consider doing that on her own, but Taylor had dismissed the idea. In her opinion children needed a father. Not that women couldn't raise kids successfully solo, but it was tough on everybody. Taylor had gotten along incredibly well with her father, and that relationship had formed her in so many ways. A lot of her independence had come from her father's attitude toward her. He'd always told her she could do anything, be anyone she wanted to be.

She couldn't imagine having grown up without his influence.

So, okay, maybe by the time she was thirty-five, if she still hadn't found Mr. Right, then she'd seriously consider it. But for now, she was determined to go for the brass ring. Being with Ben was an important part of the equation, and she still believed with all her heart that once this week was over, her life would change dramatically. She'd be able to date with new eyes, not always comparing the men she met to Ben.

She already felt better about things. His looks, for example. Yes, it was true he was stunningly gorgeous. But she'd been able to put that fact into perspective. There were lots of gorgeous men, but frankly, she would have been drawn to him even if he wasn't so handsome.

And that was the whole point. By the time Steve and Lisa got married she would have everything about Ben in perspective, and then she would be able to move on.

It didn't hurt that the task was going to be such a pleasant one, either. She grinned, but her mood deflated the next second. Perspective was well and fine, but the end result also meant she was going to lose something kind of special. A long-held fantasy was going to disappear in the light of those new eyes, and that was kind of sad.

He'd been her superhero, her perfect guy for so long, it was hard to imagine that standard falling away. But it had to.

Someone bumped her right shoulder, and she turned to face a nice-looking, white-haired gentleman in a really snazzy tuxedo. He smiled, bowed his head gently and apologized. She nodded, then headed toward the elevator, but stopped just before she left the casino floor. There was an Elvis slot machine which would play a song if you hit the jackpot. She pulled a five from her purse, and slipped it in the slot. Instead of a handle, she pressed a button, playing maximum coins. Nothing.

Nothing the second hit, or the third. In the end she only got one cherry. Her five was gone, and she hadn't heard "Love Me Tender."

C'est la vie. Her real gamble was up in his room, sleeping by now. Dreaming of her?

BEN STARED AT THE CLOCK on the night table, the minutes passing so slowly they felt like hours. Sleep eluded him—due, to a large degree, to his preoccupation with Taylor.

The connection was still there after all these years. He hadn't expected that. She'd been so young back then, and had he had an ounce of decency in him, he'd be ashamed that he'd taken advantage of her youth. Yeah, she'd come on to him, but a stronger man would have said no. When it came to Taylor, however, he wasn't the least bit strong.

Not that he'd always felt that way about her. Back when he and Steve had first started hanging out, Taylor had been a nuisance. She'd followed them everywhere in the tradition of baby sisters, always running to her mother when they'd shut her out of their "big kid" adventures. So they'd had to drag her along when it would have been a lot more fun without her.

He hadn't minded too much. As an only child, he'd always wondered what it would be like to have a sibling. He would have voted for a brother, however. A girl was too foreign. Too girly. And he'd wanted to be the toughest kid in town.

Steve had always protected the little brat, no matter what, even though he'd complained about her presence. Then protecting Taylor had become a part of him, too. He'd kept the older kids from picking on the tall, skinny tomboy.

After he'd graduated high school, he'd pretty much forgotten about her. Until he'd come home that last week, just after she'd turned eighteen.

His folks were gone on a trip he'd bought them. He'd liked the quiet and the peace, the time to study. He'd been taking night classes, studying forensics. During the day, he'd been a beat cop, and the toll had been heavy. The week away had been a blessing.

When Taylor had dropped by, making it awkwardly, painfully clear that she'd wanted him to take her, he'd hesitated, sure, but finally, he'd given in.

They'd stayed in bed for damn near three days. Doing everything they could think of, and by God the girl had an amazing imagination. She'd been wild, free, unafraid. The first time she'd taken him in her mouth, he'd nearly had a heart attack. And he could still remember her cries when he'd showed her the pleasure of his mouth on her.

She'd cried when they said goodbye, and he'd felt bad, but he'd explained to her that he was only in town for a short visit. The letters she'd sent him had come frequently at first, always with an invitation for a return visit, but he'd only answered one. There was no future for the two of them. Even if she had ended up at a college in New York, he couldn't have kept up a relationship.

His career had been his whole focus for a long, long time. Back then, he'd wanted to be a homicide detective, and he'd accepted every lousy assignment, volunteered for all the crap no one else wanted to do. He'd eventually gotten his master's degree in forensic science.

But he'd still made it out to California most years to go fishing with Steve. He'd heard about Taylor's adventures at Berkeley, her first apartment, her job as a paralegal.

Steve had also told her that Taylor wanted to marry, to have kids, to have the kind of life that demanded the suburbs. Not Manhattan. Not with a cop.

But this week wasn't about marriage and kids, at least not for them. It was Vegas, after all. Sin City. They were here to have a good time, to be there for Steve, although not in the way Steve imagined.

Ben turned over, thinking about his friend, what had gotten into him. Lisa represented everything Steve had avoided in his life. His love of his fishing boats, and his freedom, were so important to Steve, and anyone who knew him saw that from the get-go. So what had happened? Why the radical shift?

Lisa seemed nice enough, but there was no way in hell she was going to make Steve forget about his life in San Diego. Kansas was a terrible mistake, Ben felt it in his bones.

Maybe he should just shut up and let Steve do what

he needed to. Or maybe, this was what being a friend was all about.

Whatever, he wasn't going to be any good to anyone if he didn't get some sleep.

His hand moved down his stomach until he gripped his length in his hand. Eyes closed, he pictured Taylor sitting across from him in the cabana. That tantalizing stretch of bare thigh.

Before he'd even gotten to the really good parts, it was over. He forced himself to get up, go to the bathroom, but now, exhaustion had taken over full-force. Once he was back in bed, the minute he'd plunked his head on the pillow he fell into a deep sleep.

TAYLOR DIALED BEN'S cell from the pay phone next to the Pink Taco. It rang once, and she heard his sleepy voice growl his "Hello."

"Oh, God, I'm sorry. Go back to sleep. Call me later."

"No, no. I'm up. I just haven't had coffee yet."

"Have it down here. Let's meet at the coffee shop."

"Sure. Give me about ten minutes."

"Okay. I'll get a table."

He hung up and so did she. Damn, even his voice made her twitchy. That low grumble made her want to be there in person when he woke up. She desperately wanted to see his hair tousled, the first smile of the day. Maybe tomorrow.

She brushed her hair back from her shoulder, and went looking for the coffee shop. It was called Mister Lucky's, and there was a small line of people waiting for a table. Almost everyone wore shorts and T-shirts, mostly brightly colored, although more so with the women than the men. Sandals were the footwear of choice, and the accessory of the day was small cameras, equally divided between still and video.

She had chosen her outfit with care. Khaki culottes with a nice leather belt, a pale green sleeveless cotton shirt, nothing spectacular at all, but she felt really comfortable in the outfit which was the important thing. She'd worn her angel earrings, the ones she'd picked up in Sedona two years before. They were kitschy, but she didn't care. They were her favorites.

Her gaze went toward the elevators, but she didn't spot Ben. And then she did.

He had on jeans, well-worn and perfect, with a navy polo shirt. His hair was slicked back, still damp from his shower. Her stomach tightened, and she had the urge to squeeze her legs together. What he did to her had to be illegal in most states. Luckily, Nevada wasn't one of them.

He walked right to her, leaned over and kissed her on the lips, stealing her breath and her equilibrium. She put her hand on the wall behind her to steady herself, and when he smiled at her, she gripped harder.

"Morning."

"Hi."

"I hope this doesn't take long," he said. "I'm a bear before my first cup of coffee."

She cleared her throat and her head, amazed at her reaction. Sure, she wanted the guy, but to flip out completely from a pleasant peck on the lips? What would she do when he really kissed her? She'd have to make damn sure she was lying down.

"What's that smile for?"

"Nothing." She turned toward the café entrance. "It's moving pretty fast. Don't worry."

"Did you speak to your mother?"

She turned back to face him. "Yeah, I did. She's just as mystified by this whole thing as we are."

"Did she have any ideas?"

The people in front of them were led to their seats, and a moment later, a second hostess took them to a quiet table near the breakfast bar. They both ordered coffee, and didn't speak until it arrived. Ben liked his black, which made some kind of weird sense. She wondered what else he liked. Wine with dinner? Sweets?

"Okay," he said, putting his cup down on the saucer. "Where were we?"

"You asked if my mother had any ideas. She did, but she's not sure what to make of it all. About six months ago, they had dinner together, and Steve got real maudlin talking about Dad. He was beating himself up over disappointing Dad by not taking over the business."

"Your dad didn't care."

"I know. But obviously, Steve didn't get it. I think going into business with Lisa's dad is his way of making things right."

"It can't work."

"Of course not. But I don't think Steve's thinking too clearly about that."

Ben drank some more coffee, staring just past her

shoulder while he thought. The waitress came by, and he ordered eggs and bacon. She chose a cheese omelet. After refilling their cups, they were alone again, but Ben didn't say anything.

She waited, not wanting to interrupt.

Finally, he looked at her. "We need a plan. I don't want to alienate Steve, and I don't want to hurt Lisa. But we've got to do something."

She nodded. "I've been thinking about it all morning. What if we just talk to him? Tell him our concerns?"

Ben nodded. "That'll be me. Maybe give him a couple of beers to soften the blow."

"I'd like to talk to Lisa. Find out if she realizes what she's getting into."

"That should be fun."

"Oh, yeah. A real walk in the park."

The food came, and for the first few minutes, it was all business. Ben liked his toast with jam, and his eggs over-medium. She watched him while she ate her omelet, liking the way he chewed. Amazed that he could even make that sexy.

When he'd downed about half his breakfast, he smiled at her. "So talk to me."

"What?"

"Talk. Tell me about your life in the city by the bay."

That caught her by surprise. She had to reshuffle the deck in her head, pull out the cards she wanted to play. "I like my job," she said. "I'd thought about going back to school, getting my law degree, but honestly, I don't want the headaches. I like the research a lot, which I didn't expect. I work for a major law firm. They pay me well to look up the right statutes, dig on the Internet. I imagine in that way, our jobs are similar.''

"Sounds like it. You hang out with attorneys?"

"Not if I can help it. I have a small but eclectic group of friends. I play pool on Thursday nights."

His brows rose. "No kidding?"

She grinned. "We got the league championship last year, and we're gunning for it again. We have a good team."

"Eight ball?"

"Yep. Sometimes nine ball. But mostly eight."

"Maybe we can find a pool hall somewhere nearby."

"Actually, there's a place across from the Rio. It's called Pink-ees. Great place to play. Lots of tables."

"Did you bring your cue?"

She shook her head. "Didn't know if there'd be time."

"Let's make time."

She took a bite of toast to hide her ridiculously happy grin. He liked pool. Excellent.

"So what else?" he asked. "Besides being a pool shark?"

"I ride my bike on weekends a lot."

"You said you have a Shadow, right?"

She nodded.

"What got you into that?"

"A guy I went out with. He was kind of a dick, but he did turn me on to bikes. I got hooked immediately."

"Not afraid you'll get hit?"

"Nope, not really. I operate on the principle that everyone's trying to kill me."

He laughed, and she felt all squishy inside.

"What about you?"

"Yeah, I think people are trying to kill me, too."

"No, I meant what you do. When you aren't being a private eye."

He frowned a little, two lines appearing on his forehead. "I read too much."

"How can anyone read too much?"

"Trust me, it's possible."

"What kinds of books?"

"Everything."

"I doubt that."

He grinned. "Okay, so I'm not real big on romance novels. Or fantasy. But pretty much everything else."

"Cool."

"And I hike."

"Where?"

"Wherever I can. I go out to the Catskills from time to time. And upstate New York. There are some nice places in Connecticut and Vermont, too."

"How strenuous."

"Have to be able to run. Remember, people trying to kill me and all that."

She leaned forward. "Has anyone really?"

"Tried to kill me? Yep."

"Oh, God."

"They didn't succeed."

"Obviously. Why?"

"I was faster. From all the hiking."

"No, why did they try to kill you?"

"I found out stuff they didn't want known."

"Scary."

"Yeah. I try to avoid that kind of thing, but sometimes you get surprised."

"That's not the kind of surprise I like."

"But you do like surprises?"

She nodded. "Love 'em. Especially when there are gifts involved."

He laughed. "Hey, let's finish up here. I'm starting to feel lucky."

She quirked her head to the right, but he was busy with the check. She wondered if his idea of feeling lucky involved a locked door, a bedroom and getting naked.

4

_____

THE CASINO WAS HOPPING, tourists and locals all focused on winning the big one, the one that would change their lives forever. Ben knew the odds of that happening were slim to none, but he didn't care. He wanted to play, and to watch Taylor.

"You like blackjack?" he asked.

She nodded. "The last time I was here, I won two hundred dollars. I spent the whole wad on a pair of shoes that hurt my feet."

He grinned, took her hand. "Let's see if we can get another pair." He led her past the machines, surprised as always at the silliness of the glorified tic-tac-toe slots: Little Green Aliens, The Beverly Hillbillies, Elvis and The Munsters, just to name a few. Then they hit the banks of video poker machines, which was a little more understandable, but still confusing. If he was going to play poker, he wanted to do it with other people, preferably in someone's basement, with plenty of beer, sandwiches and good cigars.

Now blackjack, he liked. The only exception to that was when some obnoxious twit came to the table. He'd walk away before he'd play with a drunk who hit on seventeen, and doubled down on face cards.

They had to pass three tables before they found one with two open seats. He got Taylor in position, then sat on the stool next to her. Rubbing the smooth green felt, he checked out their compatriots. An older couple in brightly colored Hawaiian shirts, a tall gaunt man with a three-day stubble and hooded eyes and a young woman who didn't look old enough to drive, let alone gamble.

The dealer's name was Angel, and her name tag said she was from Tucson. She'd already dealt a hand, and was now going around the table, taking everyone's bets, as she'd hit twenty-one in five cards.

Ben got out his wallet and pulled out a hundred. He laid it down above the rectangle where he'd place his own bet.

Taylor reached for her purse, but he stopped her. "This one's on me," he said. "For luck."

Her eyes narrowed. "Are you sure? I brought fun money."

"You'll have plenty of time to spend it. I promise."

"All right. Thank you."

Angel took his bill, laid it out flat in front of her, so the security cameras could get a good shot, called out, "Change one hundred," for the benefit of the pit boss, then gave him a stack of five, ten and twenty dollar chips. He split them up, fifty-fifty and gave Taylor her share.

She smiled again, making him want to give her all the money in his wallet, then she put a five, the minimum bet, down to play.

He did the same.

The dealer, taking the cards from the shoe, dealt the hand, and after the second card, Taylor gasped, turned over her cards to show a jack and an ace.

The dealer paid her, took her cards, then went on with the rest of the hand. Ben had a twenty, so he stayed pat. He leaned over to Taylor, getting a heady hit of her delicate scent for his trouble. "See, I told you we were going to be lucky."

She turned to face him, her expression serious, but with a telltale gleam in her beautiful blue eyes. "You have no idea."

His whole body reacted to her message, and it was all he could do not to leave the money, the cards, his dignity on the table and drag her up to his room. But he was strong, dammit. He wasn't a teenager, run by his hormones. Half the fun was the seduction, and he wasn't about to give short shrift to what promised to be the best week of his life. He'd wait. He'd play. And in the end, they'd both win.

The next round went by in a blur, but since the dealer busted, they both won.

The woman sitting to his left smiled. "Where are you two from?"

Before Taylor could speak, he nudged her lightly with his elbow. "Home base is London."

"Really?"

He turned slyly to Taylor and gave her a wink before facing his neighbor again. "Yes."

"You don't have a British accent."

"We're trained not to."

She blinked. "Oh."

"I'm James," he said, holding out his hand. "And this is Jinx."

He heard Taylor cough, which he assumed was a cover for laughter. She didn't know that this was a game he played frequently, making up some ridiculous persona when the truth would have done just as well, but less amusingly.

"I'm Sarah," she said. "I live in the Valley. That's in Southern California."

Ben nodded. "Ah, yes. The heart of the pornography industry."

Sarah's cheeks reddened. "I wouldn't know about that."

"Of course not."

"I work for a post-production house. But not that kind."

"Fascinating."

The cards went out again, and until the payout, the conversation ebbed. Taylor took the opportunity to elbow him.

"What are you doing?" she whispered.

"Having fun," he whispered back.

"So you fancy yourself Bond, eh?"

"Hey, I could have called you Pussy Galore."

"I would have decked you if you had."

He grinned. "Hey, she was a real character."

"Only a man would say that was a *real* character."

"Sir?"

He looked up at Angel, waiting for him to hit or stand pat. His cards, a six and five, were a surprise. He doubled down, and she hit him with a king. Twenty-one.

Taylor didn't say anything, just gave him a smile. But as the rest of the hands were played, he felt something at his ankle. It was Taylor's foot. She'd slipped off her shoe, and was using her bare toes to tease him. It worked.

He glanced at her, but the smile had become a sly grin, and her gaze had shifted to Angel, watching her shuffle as if it mattered.

Ben said nothing, just enjoyed the feeling of her toes. He'd never been a foot man, but at the moment, he could understand the impulse. It wasn't easy to stay still, and not touch her thigh and run his hand over that smooth skin. The image of her on his bed, naked, him holding her by the heel as he studied her pink painted nails, took hold of him and didn't let him go until Angel coughed.

He picked up his cards, a ten and a seven, then slipped them under his ten-dollar bet. He didn't give a damn if he won or not. The only thing that mattered at the moment was the woman next to him.

Just as he was about to suggest they leave, a waitress came by. She was young and pretty, as were all the cocktail waitresses in the hotel. Taylor turned to her. "I'll have a Bloody Mary," she said. "He'll have a martini. Shaken, not stirred."

He laughed. The waitress jotted the orders without so much as a blink, then got the rest of the drink orders. So Taylor liked his game.

He faced Sarah. "Are you here by yourself?"

She shook her head. "I'm with three friends from work."

"And they are…?"

"At the pool. But I burn so easily, it seemed kind of dumb."

"This is more interesting," he said. "You can learn a lot about people by watching them gamble."

"Really?"

"See that man at the Wheel of Fortune?"

She followed his gaze and nodded when she saw the portly fellow standing next to his stool, feeding a bill into the machine. He didn't look as if he was having a very good time. In fact, his heavy brows furrowed to match his scowl, his scalp, bald all the way back to the crown of his head, was beaded with sweat. His light cotton shirt was stretched across his ample beer belly, and there were large circles of sweat under his arms. He ignored the pull lever, pushing the maximum-bet button with the palm of his hand. As the wheels spun, his lips moved. Probably a prayer, and then a curse as he got nothing, nothing, nothing.

"He isn't having much luck," Sarah observed.

"No, it doesn't appear he is. You know that every time he pushes the button, it's two dollars."

"Oh."

"And since we've been watching him, he's pressed that button what, twelve times? That's twenty-four dollars. He was standing there before we sat down."

"Whoa, that's a lot of money."

"He's not holding a bucket, so no winnings."

"Yikes."

"Indeed. What else do you see?"

While Sarah studied the scene, he turned to Taylor. "You realize, of course," he whispered, "you're not going to get away with this unscathed."

"What?" she asked, batting her eyelashes like the soul of innocence while she inched her toes up his calf.

"Whatever you had planned this afternoon? Cancel it."

Her cheeks became pink and the gaze that met his was full of anticipation and excitement. "I don't know," she said. "I have to meet my mother."

"Meet her later."

"You presume, Mr. Bowman."

He looked at her for a long moment. Then he leaned over so his lips were an inch from the soft shell of her ear. "I'm going to make you beg for mercy."

She inhaled sharply, grabbed her cards with trembling fingers.

Sarah, to his left, said, "Hey."

He held back his grin as he turned to his young friend. "Yes?"

"He's got a whole bunch of glasses stacked there. And he's kind of swaying," Sarah said.

"Which means?"

"He's toasted. And scared. He's lost a whole bunch of money and he's trying to win it back."

"Excellent."

"Cool."

"It pays to be observant."

It was Sarah's turn to grin. "Like seeing that you two aren't from London at all. That you've been playing footsie for about ten minutes, and that while I'm not positive your name isn't James, it sure as heck isn't Bond."

Taylor laughed. Angel grinned, and it wasn't because she'd dealt herself twenty-one.

"Very good, Sarah. If you ever get tired of post-production, you'd make a good detective."

She smiled, mightily pleased with herself. "Is that what you really do?"

He held out his hand. "Ben Bowman, Private Detective."

She shook his hand, but her gaze went to Taylor. "Are you a P.I., too?"

"I'm a paralegal, which isn't half as interesting."

"Somehow, I doubt that."

"Are you playing, sir?"

Ben realized he'd abandoned his cards altogether. He slipped two five dollar chips into the rectangle, and put another five above it, playing the bet for the dealer.

Taylor and Sarah both straightened, made their own bets, and each of them followed suit in tipping Angel. It turned out well for everyone. Angel busted with twenty-four.

"It's almost noon," Taylor said. "My mother's going to be here in an hour."

He shoved his whole stack of chips toward the center of the table. "Cash me in, please."

Taylor's laughter was as intoxicating as the drink that arrived while he waited for his chips.

"Still want to cash out?" Taylor asked.

"Oh, yeah."

"But our drinks..."

"Are portable."

"Good point."

Sarah sighed. "You guys are so lucky. How wonderful to be in love in Las Vegas."

Ben froze, Taylor cleared her throat and Angel wasn't at all successful in hiding a knowing grin.

Taylor pushed her chips in after Ben got his money back. "We are lucky, thank you. But we're actually here for my brother's wedding."

Sarah leaned forward over the lip of the table. "Why not make it a double wedding? Or better yet, run off to one of those cool chapels. You could get married by Elvis." She reached frantically into her oversized purse and pulled out a small notebook and a pen. "This is my room number. I'm here for three more days. If you guys do get married, I want to be there."

"I'd be delighted to take your card," Ben said with a bow. "But I've been married. It's not going to happen again. Ever."

Sarah smiled at him slyly. "You never know. Magic things happen in Las Vegas."

He looked at Taylor. "Magic, yes. But some things aren't in the cards." Nodding once more at Sarah, he said, "Hope you win a bundle."

She glanced back at the Wheel of Fortune. The same man was still desperately pressing the max bet button, the only thing to have changed was the number of empty cocktail glasses beside him. "I'll settle for not losing my shirt."

"Good girl."

"I'm ready," Taylor said, and from the high flush of her cheeks, he believed her.

Sarah was forgotten in a flash, as was blackjack,

gambling of any sort, the casino, the hotel, the entire
city. All that mattered was the woman in front of him
and getting her to his room. There was so much to
do.

He took her arm at the elbow. "Let's go."

TAYLOR PRACTICALLY had to run to keep up with
Ben's long strides. He darted and weaved through the
crowd, aiming for the elevators. Her drink sloshed as
she tried not to step on toes. It would have been
smarter just to put the glass down, but there was no
stopping Ben. Nor did she want to. She felt like a
teenager.... No, like the teenager she'd been with
Ben. How she'd loved him! He'd been the only thing
in her life for well over a year.

She sidestepped to avoid a woman in a wheelchair,
her purse banging into her side, then they were clear
of the casino.

Ben looked back at her, and his grin made her toes
curl. She didn't know the specifics of his plan, but
she was all in favor of the general idea.

Good thing she'd dressed with care this morning;
shaved everything that should be, worn her matching
pink lace bra and panties. She'd even put a couple of
condoms in her purse. Then she'd written to her
friends at Eve's Apple, filling them in on the distinct
possibility that her Man To Do would be Done before
tomorrow. She hadn't really thought it would happen
quite this soon, but who was she to complain?

Ben slowed as they neared the elevator, pulling her
close enough to slip his arm around her shoulders.

"I don't remember," he whispered, "if I told you how beautiful you look this morning."

She shook her head. "No, I don't think you did."

He nipped her earlobe. "You're stunning."

She shivered all the way down to her toes. "Why Mr. Bowman, I do declare."

His laugh added to her shivers. "I didn't know Southern California was part of the Deep South."

Finally, they were at the elevator. The button had already been pushed, but Ben pressed it again. They waited with a family of four, all wearing Las Vegas T-shirts, the adults from Caesar's Palace, the kids from Circus Circus. The littlest kid looked to be about three, and very cranky. He tugged on Daddy's shorts, whining about something named "Snooky."

By the time their elevator arrived, three more people had joined the queue and they all clambered in together, Ben guiding her to the back. He stood next to her, his hip against hers.

As they ascended, she felt a slight tickle just below the hem of her shorts. She jumped, but then realized it was Ben's fingers, brushing lightly against her skin.

With each floor, his fingers moved up the back of her thigh. She felt herself blush even though no one was looking at them. It was an incredibly intimate gesture, brazen, and yet totally discreet.

His fingers kept inching up until he brushed the curve of her buttock. Barely touching her, he swept his finger back and forth over the same small patch, giving her goose bumps everywhere. Driving her crazy.

She pressed back against the elevator wall, trapping his hand. "Stop," she whispered.

"Why?"

"Just wait."

"I don't want to wait."

"There's only one more stop before our floor."

"Then it shouldn't be a problem. Come on. Move."

She shook her head, figuring she'd won the battle.

Wrong. He turned until he was directly in front of her, his body pressed against hers so tightly she could feel his hard length, the sharp edge of his belt buckle. He smiled, his brown eyes filled with wicked intent, and then he kissed her.

Thank goodness the family had gotten off two floors down, because the kiss was definitely not G-rated. His tongue slipped between her surprised lips, exploring, darting, daring her to respond, to forget where they were, that they weren't alone.

Her hands went to his shoulders, trying to push him back, but he wasn't having any of that. Instead, he folded her in his arms, and reminded her what it was she'd loved about kissing.

His mouth opened just enough, his tongue, tasting slightly of gin, teased her into a moan that should have embarrassed her a great deal more than it did.

Then he was gone, leaving her on shaky legs, her mouth still open and moist. It took her a second to realize the elevator had stopped, that the strangers at each corner were staring at her, that Ben had already walked into the hall.

She escaped with seconds to spare.

He grinned again, knowing full well what he'd done, what he'd put her through. "I warned you," he said.

"Okay. If that's the way you want to play it." She didn't wait for his response, she just headed down the hall toward her room.

He caught up to her seconds later, putting that devil hand of his on the small of her back. "Yeah, I think it is the way I want to play it."

"No mercy?"

His pace quickened along with his heartbeat. "No mercy."

5

BEN'S THOUGHTS went immediately to the gutter. *No mercy.* The thought of taking Taylor right to the edge made his body hum with adrenaline and flat-out need.

From the moment he'd seen her last night, he'd spent every idle moment running seduction scenarios. Each vignette was rawer than the last, as the memory of that wild eighteen-year-old spurred him farther.

She wasn't eighteen anymore, but he could still see the girl in her. Made better by the years, and not just because her body had ripened to perfection. There was something whole about her, confident and sure. As if she'd grown into someone she liked very much. He couldn't remember ever thinking that about a woman, and he couldn't even give any particulars as to what had brought on the impression. The way she dressed, the way she held herself. Who cared? It was just hot as hell.

She stopped three rooms before his and pulled out her key card. It took her two tries to get the green light, but once she did, she flung the door open and dragged him in behind her.

Before she let him go, she kicked the door shut, then shoved him against the wall. He barely had time to grin before her hands were on his shoulders and her lips were crushing his.

His eyes closed as her tongue thrust into his mouth. It was her show, and he wasn't about to interfere. Not when she made full body contact, rubbing against him from breasts to hips.

If she couldn't feel what she was doing to him, then something was seriously wrong, but he figured she got the drift. Especially after she gave him the little bump and grind right where it counted.

Taylor pulled back just enough to nip his lower lip, then she was off him, walking toward the minibar.

He, on the other hand, felt like a moth pinned to a Peg-Board, unable to move. "Damn, girl. A drive-by ravishing."

She laughed, and the sound shot right to his groin. After a moment pondering the inside of the small fridge, she brought out a bottle of white wine. "It's not a martini, but would you like some?"

He shook his head. "I already had one. Too early for another."

"I know. Hey, it's Vegas. No rules."

"No mercy, no rules. What have I gotten myself into?"

She put the bottle on the dresser and her hand on her hip. "You're right. If you were smart, you'd peel yourself off that wall and march right out of here."

He chuckled as he complied with the first part, but instead of leaving, he joined her near the dresser. "I've never forgotten you," he said.

"Oh?"

Shaking his head, he moved in closer, not touching

her with his hands, but with his body. "That weekend rates right up there with the moon landing and getting my first bike."

"Wow, and I thought you were just humoring me."

"Hey, you needed a guiding hand, and God knows at that age, I was all hands."

"You sweet-talker. I'm all aflutter."

"No, you're not. But you will be." He leaned in then, touching her lips lightly with his own. He wanted to take it slowly this time, learning her with due diligence and patience. They had almost a week, and he planned to milk each step for all it was worth.

She didn't try to rush him. In fact, she simply parted her lips slightly and shared her sweet breath as he lazily ran his tongue over her silky contours.

He thought about moving to the bed, but that could wait, too. For now, the only thing that mattered was her mouth, the way she tasted, the softness and the heat.

Her body, touching him at his waist and slightly below, melted back against the credenza, but she didn't use her hands to steady herself. It was as if they had choreographed the whole scene beforehand. To test his theory he pulled back and she followed effortlessly, neither increasing or decreasing the pressure of the kiss. Damn. He thought immediately of how the principle would apply when they got to the bed. Like synchronized swimmers without the water. Maybe he should try it now, while the magic was still in the air.

He took her hand and led her through the doorway

to the bedroom. She used her index finger to tickle his palm, and his whole body reacted. Who was this woman, and how could she turn him to mush with just a single finger?

He stopped her just shy of the queen-size bed. Smiling to match her devilish grin, he ran his hands lightly up her blouse, barely lingering on her breasts. He undid her top button then pushed the material to the sides, baring a small patch of décolletage. Leaning forward, he kissed the newly bared skin, then licked her as if she'd been covered in honey. It wasn't that far from the truth. She tasted sweet and smelled like summer.

She reached up to his shirt, but he shook his head. "Not yet."

Her hands dropped obediently to her sides.

He moved down to the next button, and as he'd done with the first, he spread the material of her blouse. This time he was rewarded with a view of her delicate pink lace bra, molding her breasts into perfect soft mounds. He could just make out the slight darkness of her nipples. Part of him wanted to rip the damn thing off her, but he held back, enjoying the slow torment. He bent forward and kissed the top of her right breast, then licked his way across to the top of her left.

Her skin changed halfway there, breaking out into a field of gooseflesh. Beneath his tongue, he felt her tremble. He'd been hard since she'd touched him with her toes, but now he felt as if he would burst out of his jeans.

Still, he didn't rush. He unbuttoned her farther,

flared her blouse, exposing the fullness of her chest. He knelt a bit and kissed her underneath her bra, but that was a tease. Rising just enough, he put his mouth fully over her right nipple, hidden behind the lace. It wasn't so concealed that he couldn't feel the hardness there. He ran his tongue over the nub, slowly at first and then faster; a little demonstration of what she could expect later and not just on her breasts.

He felt her hands on his shoulder, and for a moment he thought she wanted him to stop, but when he did, she tugged him right back into place. She was simply steadying herself. Good, because he planned on being there awhile.

TAYLOR HAD DIED and gone to heaven. At the very least she was at the gate. Ben swirled his tongue around her left nipple, the lace making the sensation sort of dappled, if that were possible. She didn't care what it was called as long as he didn't stop doing it. His methodology was something he'd clearly learned over the years, because he'd been anything but patient that weekend. This was good. Very, very good. Her head lolled back as she drowned in the ocean of pleasure. It was wickedly hard not to touch him, to stand not so idly by and let him do all the work. But that was just manners talking, and this had nothing to do with etiquette.

No mercy. No rules.

It was everything she'd hoped for and a side of fries. "Oh, God."

His chuckle was more a sensation of lips on flesh than a sound, and she wanted to make him do it again.

Wait, no… His teeth captured the tip of her nipple and pulled ever so slightly. Her gasp came from somewhere outside her body, but that was the only thing she wasn't present for. God, his hands were on her bare waist, tickling fingers setting her quiver factor on high.

The tickling stopped so his fingers could work on her button. Since her blouse was open, he undid her culottes. He knelt before her, found the zipper pull with his teeth and slowly pulled it down. She was grateful for the dresser, because without it she would have melted right down to the floor.

He let go of the zipper and spread the opening of her pants. It was unbelievably erotic to have him on the floor in front of her, knowing he could touch her anywhere, do anything. He kissed her, right below her belly button. Her head went back, her eyes fluttered closed and she whimpered in pure surrender. She wanted him to hurry, to rip off the rest of her clothes and throw her on the bed. She wanted him to go slower, to make every sensation last a lifetime.

Just the fact that she let him do this, let him take her wherever he wanted to go, astonished her almost as much as the feelings of need inside her. She never did this, didn't like it when she wasn't the one calling the shots, but not with Ben. Not Ben.

"Oh, God," he whispered, just before he licked the expanse of flesh just above her lace panties.

She nodded. Oh, God indeed. The thought of where he was going, what he was going to lick next, made her dizzy and a little faint. She was no Southern Belle, all swoony over being touched, but this was to "touching" like "Mary Had A Little Lamb" was to Mozart's Requiem.

Ben touched her thigh, and she realized her shorts had dropped. He used both hands, very gently and very lightly to run between her knees and the bottom of her panties. "You taste like sweet cream," he whispered.

She put her hands on his head, ran her fingers through his dark hair. "Stand up. Please."

He looked up at her and smiled. "Not yet."

"But I want..."

He got up from his knees, kissed her hard. Let his body lean against her and she felt his erection through his soft jeans.

When he finally pulled back, he stared at her for a long moment. "Why did we wait so long?"

She laughed. "We just got here last night."

"Ten years," he said. "I missed too much."

Her hand went to his face where she traced his remarkable cheekbones with her fingers. "I'm here now."

"Amazing."

"Do you want to know a secret?"

He nodded.

"I planned to seduce you. The moment I heard you were going to be Steve's best man."

"Really?"

She nodded. "I never forgot that weekend, either."

His grin turned rueful. "I'm not as young."

"I'm not, either."

"It's not the same."

"Oh, please. You're not over the hill yet." She let

her hand fall between them. "And it's clear you aren't having any...problems."

"No, no problems. I just don't have the same stamina."

She kissed his lips, ran her tongue along the crease. "Are you sure?"

"Pretty sure. But I'd be delighted to be wrong."

"I think it's time I wasn't the only one undressed."

"You're not undressed."

She kicked her shorts toward the bed. "Almost."

"Almost only counts in horseshoes."

"And nakedness." She reached for his top button and undid it.

He covered her hand while he shook his head. "Nope, not yet. I want to see you, first."

"That's not fair."

"Sure it is. Next time, you can undress me, and stare all you like."

"Next time?"

"You don't think I'm going to let the rest of this week go by without taking full advantage of the situation, do you?"

"We have work to do, don't forget."

He nodded. "I haven't forgotten. But there'll be time for both."

"Oh?"

"Absolutely. I mean, Steve and Lisa have to sleep sometimes."

"Maybe that's something we need to stop."

"Sleeping?"

"It's not the sleeping part I'm concerned about."

"Ah, you mean the sex."

"Exactly. Maybe that's why Steve wants to marry her."

"You think she's that special?"

She shrugged. "I'm completely bewildered by men's taste in women, and even more flummoxed by what they find sexy."

Ben cupped her breast, rubbed his finger over her encased nipple. "It's not very complex. We men are simple creatures. Food, drink, a soft body between the sheets."

"That's it, huh? Any soft body will do?"

"Oh, no. Not at all. And here I'll stop speaking for all men, and just speak for myself. If I don't find something intriguing up here," he touched her temple, "then I'm not interested in what's down here." His fingers moved from her head to the junction of her thighs.

"Come on, Ben, it's me. I'm a sure thing. You don't have to win me over."

"I'm not trying to."

She smiled. "And you know what? I believe you."

"Thank you."

"So don't you think it's the same thing with Steve?"

His face clouded a bit. "I'm not sure. Steve always did like a good time, but I also know he wasn't a hound dog, at least not around me. The things that most interested Steve were what they had in common. He wanted someone who would help with the fleet, who loved the sea as much as he does."

"Which is why Lisa makes no sense whatsoever."

"Right. Which means she's filling some other role. One he's never expressed before. At least to me."

"Me, neither."

"So in order to find out if this really is the mistake we think it is, we need to find out what Lisa represents to him. What need she's filling."

"You don't think it's just about my dad? About making things up to him?"

Ben shook his head. "No, I don't. I think there's something else going on. We talked about the situation with your dad, and Steve never seemed that upset about it. Not enough to leave the sea."

"Yeah, I know. But if not that, what?"

Ben pulled her close against him. "That's what we're going to discover. But not right this second."

"No?"

He didn't answer her. Not with words. Instead, he kissed her again, slipped his arms around her back and in one of the smoothest moves since Rhett carried Scarlet up the staircase, he undid the clasp of her bra.

While his forward flank teased her tongue unmercifully, his side troops moved into position, which wasn't exactly fair. Of course, she wasn't complaining all that strongly, not when his hands were caressing her bare breasts. Her nipples were so taut they were like little weapons themselves, but she felt pretty darn sure Ben could take care of himself.

He certainly knew how to take care of her.

"Now," she said. "My turn."

"It's all your turn, Taylor," he whispered, his lips a breath away from her own. "What gives me pleasure is to give you pleasure."

Her heart sank a tiny bit. Not that she didn't believe him... All right, she didn't. It wasn't as if she thought he was being intentionally insincere, but come on. A guy who's only pleasure is to give the woman he's with all the goodies? Didn't happen. Not outside of the movies.

"Let me make you happy," he went on, still stirring their breath together as he spoke. "Let me see the rest of you."

"I've seen me. That won't make me happy at all."

He grinned. "Ah, but I bet what I do after I see you will."

"Ah."

He kissed her again. "Come with me."

She leaned back, looking him in the eyes. "You must be good."

"Just wait. You'll see." He took her hand in his, and led her to the bed. Moving behind her, he took her blouse from her shoulders, and while she couldn't see him, she could hear the soft wisp of cloth on cloth as he folded the shirt. Then he slipped her bra off, leaving her in nothing but her panties. He sat on the bed when it was time to remove those.

First, a kiss on her belly, that damn pooch she tried so hard to lose. It would have been so nice, especially at a time like this, being naked and all in broad daylight with a man she'd craved for ten years, if she could have looked a bit more like the girl he'd seen naked before. His smile was nice, and his hunger clear in his gaze, but still, she felt sure he would have been even hungrier if her stomach had been flat.

His next kiss, slightly lower, chased all thoughts of

vanity and flat stomachs straight out of her mind. No longer able to stand idle, she found her fingers skimming through his thick, dark hair. She wanted to do much more. Kiss him, get him all naked, see everything there was to see, and then play to her heart's content. But this had its advantages, too.

Like the way his hot breath felt on that little space of skin just above her low-cut panties. Like how he trailed that breath down and down, inch by inch, while his fingers, poised on the sides of her underwear, lowered the lacy material at that maddening pace.

Soon he was past the bare skin, and his lips brushed over her small patch of pale curls. Of their own accord, her legs spread half a step apart, giving him broader access, and herself a stronger sense of balance. She had the feeling she'd need it.

A second later, he kissed her at the very top of her lower lips, and she shivered with anticipation. This was very high on her personal hit parade. A man who knew how to use his mouth for more noble purposes was a man worth knowing.

Turns out, Ben knew. Oh, God, how he knew.

By the time he was finished showing her just how much he knew, she was flat on her back on the bed, arms and legs akimbo, gasping for air, quivering like a harp string that had just been masterfully, patiently, persistently plucked.

6

IF BEN DIDN'T DO something soon, he was going to be one very embarrassed man. But it was impossible to move his gaze from the vision before him.

Taylor's chest rose and fell, making those exquisite breasts quiver ever so slightly. The sheen on her sleek body, the way she lay so abandoned and free made him think of a colt just back from a long, exhilarating run in the fields. She was a wild creature...still. He smiled, terrifically glad that some things hadn't changed.

His gaze moved back to her face, to the flush on her cheeks and neck, to her parted lips, to her blond hair floating on the bedspread like a cloud. And then his problem reared its head, so to speak. The constriction in his pants was beyond serious, nearly terminal. The last time he'd been so hard without doing anything about it was in college. He'd figured out a way to escape to a bathroom back then, but this was a different type of quandary. He wanted to make love to her, to come inside her. But he'd have to get up, go down the hall to his room, get his condoms, come back, then strip. No possible way he was going to make it off his knees without exploding. Maybe if he stopped looking at her.

His gaze shifted to the bedside table, where he saw the red light blinking on the phone. She must have had a call earlier, because the phone hadn't rung since they'd been in the room. Or maybe it had, and they just had been too involved to notice.

A second later, his hip vibrated and his own cell phone rang. No musical ditty, just a plain ring, which was annoying enough. He ignored it. Until Taylor's phone rang again.

Her head came up off the bed. "What...?"

"I guess they're trying to find us."

"Damn," she whispered as her head flopped back. "I suppose we should answer."

"They can wait."

She turned, opened one eye to look at him. "You're still dressed."

"Yep."

"Why is that?"

"I have no idea." His phone rang again, then hers, the disparate pitches mildly grating.

She crooked one finger, inviting him next to her. He stood carefully, wincing at the painful pressure.

"If I had any energy at all, I'd rip those clothes right off you."

"Aha. So my plan worked." He laughed evilly and waggled his eyebrows.

"What, so you could have your way with me? Too late."

"Oh, yeah." He put one knee on the bed, leaned over and kissed her tummy.

Her hand went to his head and she fingered his hair. "That was amazing," she whispered.

"For me, too."

"And yet..."

He chuckled. Her phone jangled once more, the ring cut off as the caller hung up. Whoever was trying to reach him hadn't been as persistent. "Are you sure you're ready for round two?"

She nodded, although her eyes were closed, and she looked like she was more ready for a nap than lovemaking.

Ben wanted to stretch out next to her, but the issues hadn't been settled. The condoms. He was here, and they were all the way in his room. He should have put them in his wallet, like the old days. But he'd never thought the morning would turn out this way.

"What are you grinning about?"

"Just thinking what a lucky guy I am."

"And here I thought I'd won the prize."

He gave in to the immediacy of needing to touch her and lay down, his head on her hair. He took in a deep breath, smelling the sweet fruity scent, the intoxicating musk from her lower body. "You didn't believe me, did you?"

"Believe what?"

He ran his hand up her stomach until he cupped one of her perfect breasts. "That giving you pleasure is what turns me on."

She smiled. "That's a wonderful philosophy, Ben. Truly."

"But..."

"No, that's all. If that's how it is for you, yippee!"

He chuckled, and took the hand closest to him and

guided it to his jeans. "Maybe this will make you a believer."

"Whoa," she said, her voice breathy. "That's got to be uncomfortable."

It only took him a second to realize he'd made a mistake. The problem increased by one hell of a lot. He squirmed under her fingers.

She released him, then turned onto her side. "Stay," she said, as if he were a puppy. Then she undid his belt, and with a look of total concentration, started on his buttons.

Every move was an experience in the pleasure-versus-pain principle. It hurt so damn good. By the time she reached the last button he was ready to explode. Which would at least eliminate the need for the condoms, but would be a definite blow to his ego.

She spread his fly open, then carefully reached inside his jeans until she held him in her palm. He hissed as she pulled him free, giving him one kind of release only to put him into a more complex kind of restraint.

"Oh, my," she whispered. "That's very impressive."

He said, "Thank you," through clenched teeth. He'd grabbed the bedspread in his fists, tried to anchor his body in some way that would keep him grounded, but when she sat up, scooted down, and bent over him, he abandoned all ties to the earth.

Her warm lips hovered an inch away when her phone rang again. His followed an instant later. Taylor looked at him guiltily, and with every ounce of strength he had, he said, "You'd better get it."

She looked down once more, and he saw her frown. But the phones were persistent as hell, and for all he knew, something was wrong. He'd feel like a dog if it were an emergency and he stopped her from getting the message.

"I'll be right back." She grabbed the phone. "Hello?"

Ben ignored his cell and struggled to sit up, then get off the bed. With what little dignity he could muster, he fled to the bathroom to try and get himself together. There would be time for stage two soon enough. If, of course, he didn't die first.

"WHERE HAVE YOU BEEN?"

Taylor looked at the closed bathroom door. "Hi, Mom. When did you get in?"

"Over an hour ago, and we've been trying to reach you ever since. Didn't you hear the page?"

"No, I'm sorry. I didn't. I was in the bath."

"For an hour?"

"Reading," she said, knowing it sounded lame. She had to turn away, to stop thinking about Ben and the state she'd left him in. Poor guy. He looked like he was hurting. She'd make it up to him. That made her smile.

"Well, get dressed and come to my room. I'm in 1012. We have to talk."

"Is everything all right?"

"Aside from the fact that Lisa and her mother are taking us to some mystery location tonight after dinner? We're supposed to be semidressed, whatever that means. And I just found out that her mother's dress is pale blue with white lace, which sounds exactly like my dress, so now I have to go buy another one, and I have no intention of spending the kind of money they charge at the hotels. So you'll have to come with me now so we can get back in time for dinner.''

''Me?'' Taylor asked, knowing it was a silly question. Her mother hated to shop, never trusted her own judgment. When Taylor had lived with her, she'd had to accompany her mom on all clothes shopping trips, and after she'd gone to San Francisco, her mother's friend Beverly had taken over the task. Normally, Taylor didn't mind, but she didn't want to leave the hotel now.

Her gaze went back to the bathroom door. Still closed.

''Please, honey, I want to talk to you about this whole mess. And who knows when we'll have time alone.''

''Sure, Mom. No problem. I'll be ready in about fifteen minutes, and I'll come by your room. Okay?''

Her mother sighed. ''Thank goodness. I'm just so...''

''Get some wine out of the minibar.''

''It's three o'clock. What are you talking about?''

''It's okay, Mom. I promise. It'll calm you down. Besides, it's Vegas. No one will think a thing about it.''

A quiet ''Humph,'' was her only response, and then the dial tone.

Fifteen minutes and she'd have to face her mother. Which meant she had to get into the shower, pronto. Maybe Ben could wash her back.

No. Fifteen minutes wasn't nearly enough time for that. She'd have to wait until later. Until tonight.

BEN WAITED FOR STEVE at the lobby lounge, debating whether he should drop a few bucks into the video poker machine imbedded in the bar. His beer was cold, he was early, so what the hell? He took out a twenty and fed it to the hungry machine.

He played double-double poker, one of the many variations of the game available on the machine. This one had no wild cards at least, and it was played like regular poker. The difference was in the payout schedule, and since it was highly unlikely that he would win, he didn't give it that much thought.

What he hadn't been able to stop thinking about was his afternoon with Taylor. Good God. He felt as if he hadn't been with a woman in years, not months. And that he hadn't been with a real woman since he'd last been with her ten years ago.

It should have told him something that he hadn't been as excited about sex with Alyson. Maybe he blanked it out, maybe he assumed it would get better. It hadn't. In fact, toward the end, the sex had disappeared completely. Of course, he was the only one who'd done without. Alyson had been with Gail, the woman who was now her life partner. And he hadn't suspected a thing.

Some private dick. Couldn't even tell that his own wife was gay. It did appease him somewhat that she hadn't known, either. Or at least she hadn't admitted it to herself until after they were married. And he did know she loved him. Just not the way a husband and wife should.

There had been women after her, of course. In the beginning, he'd been something of a jerk, proving himself, he supposed. But that had calmed down, and in the past year there had only been the occasional liaison, nothing serious, nothing earth-shaking. Just pleasant conversation, nice naked tumbles, don't let the door hit you on the ass on your way out.

With Taylor, it was anything but pleasant. Or ordinary. And he sure as hell didn't want to see anything hit her on the ass, with the possible exception of his palm.

She'd lit him up like a Roman candle, and they hadn't even done the deed. God, he wished he knew where the women had gone off to tonight. More importantly, when they'd return. He planned to be there when Taylor got back, and he didn't plan on doing much sleeping after.

In the meantime, he had to put all thoughts of the delicious Taylor out of his mind. He had Steve to himself tonight, and he planned to talk to the man. Understand what he thought he was doing. Maybe even get Steve to reconsider. At the very least, postpone.

Ben took another sip of his beer, then hit max play. He had three deuces, which he held. He almost spit when the fourth one hit. That was a damn big payoff for quarters. Maybe his luck was changing. Maybe…

He slammed the cash-out button. That's the kind of thinking that led to overspending, cash advances, trouble in River City. Not for him.

"Hey, buddy. What have you got there?"

"Stevie!" Ben turned and shook his hand the way they always did, brutally. In the old days, they'd try and break bones, but things had improved with time. Now, they just went for bruises.

Steve sat down on the stool next to Ben's. "Barkeep, I'll have one of those," he said, pointing to Ben's beer. "And get my fine friend another."

"So, tell me. What's the big secret with the girls? Why all the hush-hush stuff?"

Steve shrugged as he eyed the others nearby at the bar, his gaze lingering on a tan brunette with a very low-cut blouse. "Don't have a clue. The whole evening was set up by some friends of Lisa's back home. They couldn't make it to the wedding, so they planned this mystery evening."

"But only the women?"

"Probably something at a beauty shop. Lisa can't get enough of having her nails done, or facials or some such nonsense. She roped me into a facial once. Thought it was the most horrible thing I'd ever been through. I'd rather face gale-force winds without a rudder."

Ben chuckled at the thought, wondering again what in hell Steve was doing with Lisa Caton. "So you're giving it all up, eh? The freedom of the seas for a necktie and three-martini lunches?"

Steve nodded, his smile quizzical and his gaze fixed on the bartender. "I know you all think I've gone round the bend, but I swear I haven't. She's really something. Once you get to know her, you'll get it."

"I believe you."

"I mean, she has such a clear vision of her future. Mine now, too, I suppose. And I have to tell you, Ben, I like the picture she's painted. Sure, I'll miss the fleet, but Jesus, what kind of a life was that, I mean, long-term? You know what I'm saying?"

"No."

"Come on. Did you really think I'd be out there fishing forever? That I'd be some old geezer trying to catch sailfish for tourists?"

The beer arrived, and Steve paid for both drinks. He left a five as a tip, then turned back to Ben. "It's a damn hard life, Ben. You've been with me often enough to know that."

"Yeah. I've also been with you often enough to know that you love it. That you've never wanted to do anything but sail and fish."

"For God's sake, everyone's acting like I'm giving up the throne. It's fishing. And I'll still own the boats. I can go any time I want."

"Between selling aircraft parts, you mean?"

"You don't think I can do it?"

Ben held up his hand. "No, man. That's not what I said. I think you can do anything you set your mind to. I was in school with you, remember? You didn't even have to study half the time."

"Yeah, well, that's what I think. I can do it. Make a good living. A great living. I can take care of Lisa, and our kids. Have a life that's worth something."

Ben nodded then stared at the flashing light from his video poker machine. As if summoned, the bartender came back with his winnings, counted it out and waited somewhat obviously for a tip. Ben obliged. When he turned back to Steve, his friend's face had become sullen and his gaze far too distant. Something else was going on with this marriage thing, but…Steve wasn't about to admit what. Not outright. At least, not on one beer.

Maybe the guy didn't even realize what had compelled him to move so fast. To run as far as he could away from the sea. But Ben wasn't about to let the wedding take place unless he knew, for a fact, that Steve understood his real reasons, and still wanted to move forward.

"So, tell me about Taylor," he said.

Steve grinned, crooked his head in Ben's direction. "Tell you what?"

"What's the deal? How come she's not married with 2.3 kids and a golden Lab?"

"Hell if I know. She's had chances. I know two guys right off the bat that wanted her like crazy. Renny was an attorney, looked just like Richard Gere. He came down to San Diego and tried to get in with Mom. I guess he thought if the family approved, Taylor would cave."

"And, yet, they're not married."

Steve shook his head. "I asked her what it was about him. She told me she didn't like his hands. I know. Crazy. His hands. The guy was already pulling in high six figures. I wouldn't be surprised to see him in politics some day."

"And what about the other one?"

"Oh, shit. Yeah. What was his name? Johnny. Or Jimmy. Something like that. He loved to fish. He caught a couple of world-class barracudas on the *Silver Mermaid*. He was in finance. Arbitrage, I think. Another one who made a fortune, but our girl doesn't seem to care much about that.''

''No, I guess she doesn't.''

''Who can tell with Taylor? She could be a first-rate attorney herself, but she doesn't want to. She likes being a paralegal. Likes not having the responsibility.''

''I admire her for understanding herself so well.''

''If she really did understand herself, she'd be married by now.''

''Why do you say that?''

''That's what it's all about, right? When you get it, then it all falls into place. The people you need to meet are just...there.''

''This from the man who once told me that life was like fishing? Sometimes the net is full and sometimes the net is empty. But you still get out in the trade winds.''

Steve burst out laughing. ''Yeah, that was me all right. I think we'd been drinking kamikazes at the time, however. Quite a few of them.''

Ben smiled. ''Oh, yeah. And we met those twins. Oh, man, what were their names? Helga and Lena?''

''Helga and Leanne. Damn, were they fine, or what?''

Steve chucked him in the shoulder. ''Incredible. Amazing stamina.''

''They weren't the only ones.''

''Was it Helga who had the tattoo?''

Ben nodded. ''The snake with the big eyelashes.''

"I don't think I'll ever forget where she had that bad boy."

Ben held up his beer for a toast. "Amen." They both took generous swigs, and then Ben signaled the bartender. "The hell with this," he said. "Consider this your bachelor party, buddy. We're getting plowed."

Steve laughed, but made no protest when Ben ordered two kamikazes. Each.

TAYLOR'S SMILE started to hurt. If the spotlight hadn't been directly on her face, she wouldn't have been smiling at all. The truth was, she was mortified. Not so much for herself, but for her mother.

After all, she'd been to male strip clubs before. And the virtually naked man grinding his butt into her shoulder wouldn't have been so embarrassing if he wasn't, at the same time, giving her dear, conservative-as-tea-and-white-toast mother a sloppy French kiss.

7

TAYLOR POURED herself another glass of the cheap champagne Mimi, Lisa's mother, had bought for the table. Unfortunately, she didn't think there was enough champagne in the hotel to make her forget where she was, and that her poor mother was dying inches at a time, although she doubted Lisa or Mimi could tell that she despised this kind of thing. The two of them, on the other hand, were having a hell of a good time, laughing, drinking, slipping bills into tiny red thongs and calling out for lap dances.

Except for her attitude toward the strip club, Mimi wasn't a surprise. Looking at her, Taylor could see Lisa in about twenty years, and it wasn't a bad thing. Good skin, light wrinkles around the eyes and mouth, but not at all saggy. Blond hair, not a dark root showing. Her figure was trim, and Taylor could easily picture her on a trendy golf course, or playing doubles at the tennis club. The mother and daughter giggled in the same way, the pitch just shy of outright annoying.

The evening had been courtesy of Lisa's best girlfriends, Tiffany and Cassie. Since they couldn't make it to the wedding, they'd arranged this bachelorette party, ensuring their seats at a round table too close to the stage. Mimi had brought some gifts from back home, and Lisa had opened them quickly, squealing with delight at the see-through nightgown, the glow-in-the-dark dildo and the feather boa.

Taylor chastised herself for her petty thoughts, but the truth was, the festivities were not to her liking, and so far, neither was Lisa.

What did Steve see in her? She'd thought that in this kind of let-your-hair-down atmosphere, she'd be able to see a new side to Lisa, something that would resemble the kind of fun-loving gal Steve had always gone for. But it wasn't so.

When Lisa wasn't whooping it up, she and her mother spent most of the time when one could talk above the music gossiping about people back home. They rarely included Taylor and her mother, and when they did, it was to ask about the wedding plans. Neither had asked any personal questions, but then, perhaps Steve had filled them in. As doubtful as that was, given Steven's penchant for minding his own business, she'd still give them the benefit of the doubt.

What had really made her crazy, however, was an undercurrent between mother and daughter that was highly suspect. Not that either of them said anything that would stand up in court, but they shared looks, secret smiles, the odd raised brow, all of it to do with Steve and the immediacy of the wedding.

One of the things that hadn't set right with her was this whole Vegas marriage. Lisa didn't strike her as the kind of girl to go for a quickie ceremony. In fact, Taylor would have bet big bucks that Lisa not only had the china patterns picked out, but that somewhere in her bedroom, she owned a large hope chest, filled with a trousseau that would have everything from Egyptian cotton sheets to Grandma's silver.

Mimi had let slip one big clue, something about presents for later. That could mean that friends were going to throw Steve and Lisa a reception once they moved to Kansas, or it could mean that there wasn't going to be one wedding, but two. The Vegas wedding was to get Steve on the hook, the Kansas wedding would be to reel him in and mount him.

Whatever, Taylor wasn't pleased. At least the show was going to be over soon. It had to be. There was a second show starting in less than an hour.

"Honey, do you have any aspirin?"

Taylor's mom had leaned over, and yelled the request in her ear. She'd had to, the music was so loud. "Hold on."

She looked through her purse and pulled out a small bottle. "Here," she said, handing it to her mother. "Take all you need."

Grasping it as if it were a lifeline, her mother, Pauline, shook out three tablets, then gave back the bottle to Taylor.

"It'll be over soon," Taylor said, shouting herself. "I promise."

Pauline smiled weakly, looked around for a waiter, gave up the hunt and downed the pills with champagne.

"Tomorrow, we'll go to the spa," Taylor said. "Get a massage."

"I thought you were going shopping with Lisa."

Taylor frowned. She'd forgotten. Or more likely blocked it out. She'd promised, in the limo drive over, to accompany Lisa on a trip to the mall to find an appropriate bridesmaid's dress. She still didn't see the reason for buying something new, but when she'd described the dress she'd brought, the long silence and uncomfortable looks had made it perfectly clear the simple gray shift wasn't going to cut the mustard.

Pauline had masterfully guided the conversation, somehow making herself unavailable for the trip, but promising Taylor's presence.

At least Taylor knew where the mall was. Her shopping trip with her mother had gone very well, for Pauline at least, and if she'd known, she would have shopped for herself at the same time.

What the hell. She took another big sip of her drink. Maybe it would be the perfect opportunity to talk to Lisa. To find out why she was so intent on marrying Steve.

The men on stage, six of them, all with rock-hard bodies glistening from some kind of body oil, all with pasted-on smiles and enormous bulges in their thongs, gathered for what Taylor prayed was the finale.

They'd begun to boogie in earnest when a picture came to her mind, as vivid as a high-definition screen image—Ben doing the old bump and grind, wearing nothing but...

Nothing.

Her face heated ten degrees, she couldn't even face the general direction of her mother, and when she reached for her champagne, the glass tipped over, spilling the bubbly all over the table and the front of her dress.

It was not her best dress. It was, however, her most conservative dress, and now it was soaked, and she'd have to send it to the cleaners or wear something far more risqué than she should to dinner tomorrow night. No, that dinner, with both families, wasn't until the night after. But still, it wasn't very pleasant sitting there with a wet lap, and very naughty pictures of Ben Bowman doing unspeakable things to her insides.

Her mother, bless her little heart, saved the day when she insisted on taking Taylor to the hotel to get into something dry. They gossiped horribly about them all the way back to the Hard Rock.

It wasn't until she stepped inside the lobby that the images of Ben returned, and she made such a hasty retreat from her mother there were probably skid marks all across the purple carpet.

By the time she got to her room, nothing mattered but Ben. Not the edges of the headache starting to form, not the still wet and sticky dress, not the fact that she was far more tipsy than she'd realized.

This, she'd gathered after trying to open her door for the third time. She finally made it in, tossed her purse on the couch, lifted her dress off in one smooth move as she made a beeline for the bedroom.

Once she was in her panties and bra, a whole new set of images came to her. Ben on his knees. Ben on the bed. She reached for the phone only to stop dead in her tracks when she saw the time.

It was past midnight. She had no business calling him at this hour. He was probably sound asleep.

And if he wasn't asleep, he was probably with Steve, and that was something she definitely didn't want to interrupt. She'd had no luck with Lisa, but perhaps Ben had made some headway. He was so easy to talk to, and Steve had never been closer to another person.

The best thing she could do would be take an Alka-Seltzer, take off her makeup, get into jammies and crawl beneath the sheets. Good God, she needed to sleep, and if she could grab a healthy eight or nine hours, she'd be ready to face whatever came her way. Which, she hoped was Ben. Coming her way, indeed.

BEN WIPED THE TEARS from his eyes, but he couldn't stop laughing. He bent over the table, gasping for breath and bumped heads with Steve doing the same thing, and that made them both get hysterical all over again.

Jeez, it was great being with the old Steve. He totally cracked him up, always had. It wasn't anything anyone else would understand, which to him was the best humor of all.

Finally catching his breath, he looked around the small bar, just a college pub with some pool tables. It was crowded and raucous, but they had killer fries and a special on vodka stingers that they'd taken up.

God, Taylor had been right about that no-rules thing in Vegas. Back home, he'd have an occasional beer with dinner, and every once in a while, he'd go for some drinks with some buddies. Most of the time, he needed his wits about him, and alcohol wasn't part of his lifestyle.

Every time he'd gone for a week fishing with Steve, though, there was plenty of booze and plenty of laughs. Steve wasn't much on alcohol, either, except for special times, like tonight.

They'd talked about the old days, the great days. In high school, they'd been terrors. Steve was the one with the real smarts, and he could have gone to any college he wanted, but that hadn't been his dream. Ben hadn't done badly, but he'd had to work for it. It used to drive him crazy that even though Steve never cracked a book, he'd still managed to ace even the toughest chemistry tests.

And, oh, the girls. They'd both been jocks, with Steve, again, outshining his poor buddy. But what the hell, it had gotten them the best damn women on campus. None of them had been anything like Taylor. If he'd ever found someone like her, he would have held on for dear life, but by the time the two of them had connected, he was deep in his life in New York, and there was no way he could have pursued anything. Besides, he'd thought Steve would have killed him if he'd ever found out.

That had been the only secret he'd ever kept from his friend. Nothing else was sacred. The conquests. The failures and triumphs, they'd shared it all. Of course, Steve had his own style of "sharing." He usually waited until whatever situation had long since gone the way of all things past, and then he'd tell Ben all about it. The only exception had been his father's death, and now, Lisa.

Ben was fairly certain there was something missing from Steve's chronicle of his courtship. But good old

Steve wouldn't be pushed. So Ben had thrown in the towel and decided to have himself one hell of a night.

"I gotta eat something, man," Steve said. "You want more fries?"

He shook his head. "Don't they make anything else?"

Steve picked up a menu that was directly in front of Ben's face. "I don't know. Let's see."

Ben grinned and opened up the plastic two page list of snacks. "Wings."

"Oh, man," Steve said, moaning in ecstasy. "Wings. You're a friggin' genius."

"I know. I am."

"Plenty of hot sauce."

"Did someone say hot?"

Ben turned his head at the very feminine voice behind him. Steve's eyes had widened, and now Ben understood why. She was a stunner. Tall, slender, with long red hair flowing over her shoulders. She was dressed in skintight jeans and a T-shirt that looked painted on. It certainly did nothing to hide her prominent nipples.

"Hi, guys. I couldn't help notice you were solo tonight."

Steve gave her a smile that had captured more than one damsel's heart. "We are, sweet thing, but this here's a bachelor party."

Her pink, glistening lips turned down in a fetching frown. "Who's the lucky guy?"

Steve lifted his drink. "That would be me."

Her smile returned as her focus turned to Ben. "So you're not taken?"

Normally, he would have considered the possibilities in front of him, but the poor girl had no idea who she was up against. "Sorry, darling. I'm taken."

Now she pouted outright. "Taken, taken?"

He nodded. "More's the pity."

She sighed, which did great things to her chest, and then put on a happy face. "Well, have fun, and tell your ladies they're damn lucky."

Ben didn't look at Steve until after the waitress had come by for their orders. When he did, Steve's expression told him he was utterly confused, and wanted an explanation, pronto.

"Is something wrong?" Ben asked innocently.

"Well, I'm thinking there's something you haven't told me..."

"Me, naw. I'm in the pink." Ben waved his hand in dismissal.

Steve leaned back, studying him carefully. "Bull. Tell me what's going on. That was a major-league babe. Probably the best damn thing you've seen in years."

"True." Shit. He should have talked to Taylor about this. Did she want it to be a secret? Did he?

"Come on, Bowman. Spill."

He debated for a few minutes, until he figured Steve would brain him if he didn't say something, and then he made up his mind. He didn't want to hide or sneak around. Everyone would deal. "I'm interested in someone."

"What? Who? When?"

"You forgot how and where."

"You've been holding out, man. Come on. Give."

He took another drink, then looked Steve in the eye. "It's nothing. Yet. Except a real strong attraction."

"No shit. This is awesome. I didn't think, you know, since Alyson... Why didn't you bring this woman?"

"I didn't have to. She was already here."

"Huh?"

He leaned forward. If Steve was gonna belt him, he didn't want him ruining the furniture. "It's Taylor."

Steve's face froze. Not an eyelash quivered, not a breath escaped. Finally, after what felt like a millennium, he blinked. "Taylor? My Taylor?"

Ben nodded slowly, watching him as if his life depended on it, which it just might.

"Well, I'll be..." Steve's gaze moved from Ben's face to his own hand. For the length of an entire Nine Inch Nails song, he didn't say another word. And then came one mother of a grin. "You and Taylor, huh? I'll be damned."

"You don't mind?"

"Why would I mind? You're my two favorite people on the planet. I think it's great."

Ben let go a breath he hadn't realized he'd been holding. "Wow."

"I'll say. So has this been going on awhile?"

"You could say that."

"No shit."

"You said that already."

"It bears repeating."

The wings arrived along with a couple of beers. If

it had been anyone other than Steve, they would have talked about the situation for a long time. But Steve figured everyone was pretty much like him, that private was private. What was excellent was Steve's obvious approval. That made things a hell of a lot easier, because even if he'd insisted they stop, Ben wasn't at all sure he would have. Or could have.

After they finished the wings, Steve reached for his wallet, but Ben put a stop to that. Then they headed back to the hotel.

It was just past two when they got there, and Ben wanted to see Taylor. Now. Luckily, Steve wanted to see Lisa. They rode up the elevator together, and when it stopped on Steve's floor, he gave Ben a massive bear hug, then looked him straight in the eyes. "Thanks, man. Best bachelor party a guy could have. I'm glad you're here. And if you hurt my sister, I'll rip your heart out."

Then he walked out and down the hall, whistling.

Ben cracked up, glad they'd been alone. At his floor, he looked at his watch. It was late. He had no business bothering Taylor at this hour.

But when he got to her room, he knocked anyway. Softly, so he wouldn't wake her. When she didn't answer, he knocked a little bit harder. He wouldn't bang on the door though. That would be rude.

HE STOOD AT THE DOOR looking so good she wondered if she was dreaming. Considering the last thing she remembered was hitting the pillow, maybe she was.

"You were sleeping," he said, his voice curling inside her like sweet smoke.

"Yeah, I was."

He turned. "I'm sorry. I'll see you tomorrow."

She grabbed his arm. "Wait. It's okay. Come on in."

He smiled, and it changed his face. He could look so tough, so rugged, and yet when he smiled, his eyes became welcoming and his lips promised wonders. "You sure?"

"Uh-huh."

He leaned forward and kissed her lightly before he stepped inside. She noticed he wasn't all that steady on his feet, and his breath gave her a clue as to how he'd spent his evening.

He made his way to the couch and sort of fell on it, expelling a big gust of air. "Whoa."

"Rough night?"

"Great night. But a little too much of it, if you know what I mean."

"I do." She joined him, curling her feet under her, and spreading her robe demurely over her legs. She'd wished she'd had time to put on a little makeup, maybe brush her hair. "Did Steve say anything?"

"He said lots. Unfortunately, nothing that gave me any insight about his marriage."

"Bummer."

"Yeah. You know him, though. He doesn't believe in spitting it out until—"

"It's too late."

"Maybe not. We still have time."

She sighed. "I hope you're right."

"What about you? What was the secret 'girl thing' you all did?"

She groaned. "Oh, please. It was horrible. We went to a strip club."

His brows rose.

"Guys. Mostly naked."

"Oh?"

"Not my idea of a swell night. At least not while I'm sitting next to Mom, who looked like she was going to pass out from embarrassment."

"Ouch."

"But Lisa and her mom sure enjoyed themselves."

"Well, I'm happy for them."

"I could have lived quite happily without it, thank you. I just get more and more confused about the whole thing. I don't know. Maybe we should just be happy for him."

"He's happy for us."

"Pardon?"

"I kind of told him we were, uh, together."

"You did?"

"He seemed pretty cool about it. Although he did warn me if I hurt you he'd kill me."

"Good old Steve."

Ben's mood seemed to shift as he studied her.

"What's wrong?"

He leaned over and kissed her, taking his time. Letting her get used to him once more. "You know what? I'm gonna go."

"Why?"

He smiled and his eyes told her there was nothing

to worry about. "Because I'm tired and I've had too much to drink."

"Okay."

"It's not that I don't want to stay. It's that I want it to be perfect."

"Oh, sure," she said, crossing her arms over her chest. "Disarm me with charm and romance. As if that's gonna work."

He chuckled as he stood. "Go back to bed. Sleep well and dream about me."

She followed him to the door. "As if I could dream about anything else."

One last kiss, a gentle caress of her cheek, her chin, and then he was gone. She closed the door, leaned against the cool wood with her very warm forehead. No way she was going to get to sleep now. She should be furious that he woke her up. And that after he woke her up, he had the temerity to leave. But she wasn't.

The feeling was familiar, even though she hadn't felt it for a long, long time. Her crush on Ben was back. With a vengeance.

8

Here's the latest, kiddies: Ben is the most amazing man in the universe. And, no, I'm not exaggerating in the slightest. When we walk together in the hotel, women stop and stare, and I swear I actually see jaws drop. Of course, men look, too, which kind of makes me a wee bit self-conscious, but I can't blame them. He's just so...

Okay, so we fooled around a little this morning. No we didn't go all the way, but I went far enough to see stars. Oh, mamma. He was so intense. God, I get the shivers just thinking about it. Too, too incredible. And then I went shopping with my mom, which was fun. After that, I got roped into this horrible evening at a male strip club, which might have been fun with you guys, but with my mother sitting beside me, I swear I would have rather been at the dentist.

I came home, thought about calling Ben, figured it was too late, went to bed. Then I was awakened by a knock at the door. You guessed it. Mr. Gorgeous himself. He was so sweet! He told my brother that we were an item. Or item-lite, I guess. Which was amazing, as I didn't think he thought—well, you know. And so I'm all jazzed and ready to continue where we'd left off, and what does Ben do? He tells me he's going to bed. In his room. Alone. Because he's had too much to drink with my brother and he wants our first, uh, I mean second time to be perfect.

Which melted me, of course, but on the other hand, here I am at 2:30 a.m. typing when I should have been having an out-of-mind experience with Mr. Bowman.

What I can't figure out is why he left. Was he telling the truth? Did he get scared? Was I so hideous without my makeup that he's rethought this whole item thing? I have no clues. Any objective comments would be deeply appreciated.

Also, and this is kind of scary, I have to admit to you, and to myself, that the crush of old is back. Only, in the past ten years it's had time to ripen. While this week looks to be one of the best (please, please, please) of my life, I think leaving is going to be hell.

Okay, hope you're all doing wonderfully, and that some of you at least have picked out your MTD! Write me back. Soon.

Love, Taylor

BEN TURNED OVER and looked at the bedside clock—three-forty-five. Just great.

He punched his pillow a few times, but it still

didn't come close to his pillow at home. He'd meant to bring it, but then he'd have looked like a perfect ass carrying it all over the airport. Not that he gave a damn.

Sighing, he closed his eyes once more, and his thoughts went right back to where they'd been a minute ago. Why had he left Taylor's room? He could have stayed. Should have stayed. So what the hell had he been thinking?

She'd bought the line about wanting things to be perfect. Which was partially true. He didn't care for the idea of being toasted when they made love. Not with her. But was that really it? It's not as if they couldn't have had a great, albeit woozy evening, then done it again when he was stone sober.

Something else was going on here and he wasn't sure what. This was a dream week for him, aside from worrying about Steve. No obligations, no commitments, no having to get to know her from scratch. It was ideal in every way, and he was nuts not to take advantage of every second.

And yet, here he was in his own room, way the hell down the hall from hers.

Was it fear? Of what? That she'd get attached? That he'd get attached? That was just nuts. Not in a week. Maybe a few months, but a week? Couldn't happen.

So if it wasn't fear, then what? Performance anxiety? Jeez, he hoped not. Prayed not, but truth be told, since Alyson, he hadn't exactly been at the top of his game. Not that he hadn't been successful with the few women he'd seen, but something lingered. Why hadn't he seen it? Yeah, yeah, she'd told him a dozen times she hadn't known herself, but that information wasn't helpful. So she'd been in denial. Obviously, so had he. And if he'd been in denial with Alyson, why not with Taylor? Not that she was secretly gay, he didn't think that for a moment. But what if there was something else? Something he should see, but didn't?

Most days he realized Alyson's sexual preference was her own business, and had nothing to do with him. This wasn't most days.

Maybe his anxiety had a completely different origin. Taylor had no way of knowing it, but that long ago weekend had been spectacular. The clouds had parted, the angels wept. They'd been magic together, and from his brief foray into the mystery of Taylor this morning, they probably would be again. Only it wouldn't be the same. Couldn't be. They were both older. Him, especially. And time has a way of changing even the best of things.

So, all right, he was being a dick. It wouldn't be the same, and so what? It would still be great. Because it would be with Taylor. She was terrific. He felt comfortable with her. More comfortable than he'd been in a long, long time.

He turned over, kicked off the blankets. Enough of this Dr. Phil crap. Tomorrow night, Taylor was his. He didn't give a damn what else happened, he just knew there was no way he was going to spend another night alone while he could be with her.

No more excuses. He'd watch his liquor intake, keep himself sharp and alert. He'd even catch a nap tomorrow, seeing as he wasn't getting any sleep tonight.

And then all bets were off. She wanted no mercy? That's just what he'd give her.

TAYLOR HAD TO ADMIT, the pale pink dress was beautiful. She turned in front of the three-way mirror, scrutinizing her butt in the tight sheath. She also had to admit that Lisa had been really nice all day. Solicitous, sweet and kind. She and her mother, Mimi, had taken her to breakfast at the buffet where Taylor had eaten too much to be trying on dresses, but if she watched herself over the next few days the pooch would be gone. There was a gym at the hotel, and she'd use it. Yeah. Right.

Well, at least she could swim. She liked to swim. The pool at the hotel was so beautiful. Did Ben like to swim?

Thinking about Ben, dripping wet, the water shimmying down his chest inch by slow inch gave Taylor a whole new reason to live.

She laughed at herself. What was she, thirteen? Yeah, that's just how she felt. Like a teenager in love. Lust. Just lust. Lust was okay. Fine and dandy. Nothing more.

What was it with women? She wasn't the only one who did this, that was for sure. See a nice guy, he shows a little interest, and it's straight to wedding invitations and planning the bedroom suite.

The whole purpose of this trip, aside from the obvious, was to play with Ben Bowman. Play like a cat with a ball of yarn. The cat didn't want to set up house with the yarn. And she didn't want to set up house with Ben.

All she wanted was to get the hell past him. Enjoy, yes, but with clear vision and a clear head. Not the rich fantasy life of an eighteen-year-old with a bad case of Ben-itis. She was a grown-up now, with a responsible job, friends, an apartment, a motorcycle.

"Taylor? Are you decent?"

She turned to the curtain. "Sure, Lisa, come on in."

The curtain squealed as it slid on the rod, and Lisa's gasp could be heard throughout the dressing room. "Oh, my God! You look fantastic! That is the most gorgeous dress I've ever seen. You simply have to buy it. I'm totally jealous, and everyone's going to be looking at you instead of me."

Taylor couldn't help but smile. "Oh, please, Lisa, that's crazy talk. You're a total babe, and in that dress of yours, your gonna be a knockout."

Lisa returned her smile, looked at herself in the mirror. She wasn't in the wedding dress, which was white, on the short side, and yet oddly conservative. It had a beautiful pearled bodice and a slightly flared skirt, and she truly was a picture in it. Now, though, she was wearing a little black number. Smart. Expensive. And it made her look like she was built like a brick house.

"For the honeymoon?"

Lisa shook her head. "Dinner, tomorrow night. Didn't Steve tell you? We're going to Picasso's at the Bellagio."

"That's like the best restaurant in Vegas."

"I know. You can wear the gray dress, right? Or do you want to look at something else?"

"No, I'll be fine. But thanks."

"Honestly, you look stunning in that. Maybe with your hair up?"

"Yeah, maybe."

"We have an appointment for you at the spa, if you want it. We can cancel if you don't, but Mom thought it would be nice to set you and your mom up for hair and nails. I would be grateful for the company."

God, why was she making this so difficult? If Lisa had been a flat-out bitch, no problem. But this nice crap? How was she supposed to combat that? "Sure. It'll be fun."

"So tell me about you and Ben."

Taylor's gaze swung from her own reflection to Lisa's. "Pardon?"

"Steve told me you and he are, um, exploring the possibilities?"

She laughed. "I'll bet fifty bucks that's exactly what Steve said."

"How'd you know?"

"One thing you're going to have to get used to about Steve. He's the worst gossip ever. I mean it. It's as if he missed the whole human interest portion of knowing people. He talks to them, and unless the conversation is about fishing, it's gone. Out of there. It's amazing."

Lisa ran her hand down her hip, eyeing herself critically. "You know, I think I'm going to sneak over to the shoe department at Neiman's and see if I can't get something a little more kicky for this dress.''

Taylor realized her faux pas. "Of course, now that he's going to be in sales, it'll be the same thing. If it's not about the business, you can forget it. He won't know if someone's married, of if they're getting a divorce. Nothing juicy whatsoever.''

Lisa smiled again. ''That's okay. I gossip enough for the both of us. And I really think you should get that dress.''

''All right,'' Taylor said, reaching for the zipper. ''I'll get it. But I have to join you over at the shoe department, because I have nothing to go with this. White sandals, what do you think?''

''Perfect. Let me call Mom and tell her we'll be another hour.''

''Great.''

Lisa stepped out of the room while Taylor changed back into her sundress. It was pale yellow with little squiggles of green. No bra, but in this dress, it didn't matter—God bless built-ins. She slipped on her flip-flops and grabbed her purse. A quick moment with her hair brush and her lip gloss, and it was off to buy shoes with the woman her brother was going to marry. A marriage that she was supposed to stop. Only, she was having a pretty hard time putting her finger on the reason why.

BEN'S HEAD NEEDED HELP, and the pain medication he'd brought with him wasn't going to do the trick. It was past noon, and somehow he'd managed to shower, shave and dress. Higher thought was out of the question. Luckily, he was in a large hotel with a large gift and sundry shop. He padded across the nice thick carpet to where he'd left his sandals, put them on, then grabbed his key card and headed for relief.

Once he got to the lobby, he realized the Hard Rock wasn't the ideal place to nurse a hangover. Normally, he liked Elvis Costello, but right now it felt like a hammer to the skull.

In the gift shop, he found a bounty of headache cures. He bought three different kinds, not sure which would prove the most beneficial. Now, the key was to get coffee and quiet. The first part was no sweat, but the second? He asked the nice young lady behind the counter.

"Quiet? Sure. You got a room?"

He nodded.

She smiled.

He understood. "Thanks."

"Hope you feel better."

"Me, too." He stopped at a hotel phone halfway to the elevator and asked for room service. He ordered a large pot of coffee, a couple of eggs and some toast. "There's a nice tip if you can get it there in five minutes."

Ben wasn't encouraged by the laughter on the other end of the phone, but at least he had water in the room. He'd start with the fizzy kind of pain reliever and go from there.

Back on his floor, he slowed down as he passed Taylor's room. He thought about knocking, but that was already happening in his head, so he let it go.

His breakfast got there twenty-seven minutes later,

and when the last bite was eaten and the last cup drunk, he picked up the phone. Taylor wasn't in. He left what he thought was a witty message, but on reflection, he thought about breaking into her room and ripping out the phone. Oh, well. She'd known him for too long to blow him off over a lousy joke. He hoped.

He walked over to the window, and took a look at Sin City during the day. Man, he could see heat waves from all the way up here. What did he expect for July? It was supposed to be around 110 degrees today. But at least it was a dry heat, right? Actually, as far as he was concerned, an oven was an oven.

It was pretty damn hot in New York now, too. Which had some pluses. A lot of people left town, and a less congested Manhattan was a better Manhattan. Despite the heat, the humidity, all the crap about New York, he missed it when he wasn't there. The rhythm of the city suited him. He hadn't even guessed at that until he got there, and now he couldn't imagine living anywhere else. Of course a summer house in the mountains wouldn't hurt his feelings. Someday.

He sighed, turned, noticed that his head wasn't pounding quite so intensely. He wondered how old Steve was hangin'. Nothing made a hangover more bearable than someone else's misery.

He called Steve's room, and on the fourth ring the man himself picked up. At least he assumed it was Steve and not a bear.

"Feeling chipper, are we, Steve?" Ben laughed at the very succinct reply. "Get in the shower and get some coffee. I'll come get you in a half hour. We'll go terrorize the casino.''

''I don't know...''

''What's wrong?''

''Wait.''

There was a considerable silence. Finally, Steve cleared his throat. ''Okay. The girls are shopping. Give me forty-five minutes. I'm gonna need it.''

''You have something for your head?''

''I'll have some coffee.''

''You know, an aspirin won't kill you, buddy.''

''I don't like them.''

''It's your funeral. Later.'' Ben hung up, and pondered his next move. The girls were shopping. He assumed Taylor was involved, which would explain her not answering the phone.

Just the thought of her stirred him. God, he wanted today to pass quickly so he could get to tonight. He hadn't been this attracted to anyone in years. Even in the beginning with Alyson, there had never been a major physical thing between them. Sure, they'd made love, and it had been great, but there hadn't been a lot of passion. He'd respected her mind, liked her sense of humor, and she tolerated him better than almost anyone. About a year into the relationship, it was clear she wanted more, so he'd asked her to marry him. It seemed like the next logical step. He'd been so damn preoccupied by his work, and she'd been completely into hers, that they didn't see each other all that frequently. And then things started to slip. He'd tried to make things right with her, but it hadn't worked. Of course, when she finally told him there was someone else, it had hurt like a mother. But things he hadn't even been aware of fell into place.

They were still friends, and he liked it that way. She seemed happy with her lady, and she encouraged him to try again. He wasn't so sure about that.

Marriage had been tough for him. Even if Alyson hadn't discovered her preference for women, he doubted it would have worked out. His focus, especially back then, was too much about the job to be fair to a mate. He couldn't count how many cops had lousy marriages. Forget about other private investigators. Only one gut came to mind, Frank Rebar, who had a great marriage, good kids, all the trimmings. So while he'd had to deal with some loneliness and a definite lack of getting some, he figured it was better this way.

Although being around Taylor made the lack of getting some feel a hell of a lot more acute. Damn, imagine having her to come home to.

He walked back to the window. Staring at the bizarre skyline, he realized it was the city talking. Vegas was Neverland for adults. It wasn't the real world, with the stresses and strains of daily life. She had a life in San Francisco, a job she liked a lot. His life was far from normal, with odd hours, dangerous people, nothing like stability.

He turned away abruptly, angry at himself for even thinking such stupid thoughts. This was a week of indulgence, that's all. It would make a hell of a memory, but it wasn't going outside the city limits. He didn't even want it to.

His life worked just the way it was. The important thing now was to make sure Steve wasn't getting himself in hot water. That's all that mattered.

That, and rocking Taylor's world.

9

"HEY. YOU'RE NOT THERE. Oh, well. I thought... Oh, I know. You're out winning a couple million, right? Try not to forget your humble roots. Uh, well, give me a buzz when you come back."

Taylor pressed the button to repeat the message, smiling stupidly as she listened to Ben's silly little message. It was goofy and sweet and wonderful. She fell straight back on her bed, spreading her arms wide, then tossed her flip-flops across the bedroom. Shopping was over, she had no plans to meet anyone from her family until tomorrow, which meant she was free-free-free to play with Ben to her heart's content. "Yipee," she whispered, not that anyone could hear her.

The phone rang and she bolted upright, grabbing the receiver before the ring finished. "Hello?"

"So, how did shopping go?"

Her spirits sank, but just a bit. "Hi, Mom. It went fine. I got a really beautiful pink dress, a bathing suit and an incredible deal on shoes and a purse."

"I'm delighted, Taylor, but I was actually more interested in how it went with Lisa."

"Oh, yeah. You know, the thing is, she was really nice."

"I didn't think your brother would pick out a shrew."

"No, but I'm still not convinced he's doing the right thing. Last night I got the impression that the whole reason for this Vegas deal was so Steve couldn't get away."

Her mother was silent for a long beat. "I know. So what's next? Do we leave it alone? Let him make what might not be a mistake?"

"At this point, I'd just be happy if they would delay things. Give him a chance to think this through."

"See what you can do, sweetie." Her mother sighed. "I'm just going to try to avoid Mimi. At least until dinner tomorrow night."

"Right."

"Do you have plans for dinner?"

Taylor winced. She should eat with her mother, it was the right thing to do. "Yep. I'm booked. I'm meeting Ben and we're going to strategize."

"Is that what you call it these days?"

"Mother!"

"Be careful, Taylor. I don't want to worry about two children."

"Everything's peachy with me, Mom. You order something decadent from room service and watch in-room movies. Or better yet, why don't you go over to the Palace Station and play bingo?"

"I just might. And I suppose I should mention that Ben and Steve are downstairs throwing perfectly good money down the toilet at the craps tables."

"Thanks. Talk to you later." Taylor hung up. She should probably leave Ben and Steve alone.

Fat chance.

BEN SHOOK the dice in two hands, resisting the urge to blow on them and say "Papa needs a new pair of shoes." Instead, he threw the dice toward the back rail of the craps table and rolled boxcars.

Steve pumped his arm twice. "Awesome."

Ben got the dice back, and rolled again. In fact, he rolled seven times before he crapped out. Both men, and several of the others standing around the table, made out like bandits. Then it was someone else's turn to roll, and Ben started gathering his chips.

"Hey, what do you think you're doing?"

"I thought I'd check up on Taylor."

"Are you kidding? They're shopping. They'll be at it 'til the cows come home."

Ben wasn't so sure about that, but he didn't mind hanging out a little longer with Steve. They could still be young and stupid together, which he missed. Back in New York he was serious all the damn time. Except for his weekly pickup game at the Y, he didn't do squat to have fun.

He let go of his chips and took advantage of the nearby cocktail waitress, ordering a soda for himself and a beer for Steve.

When he turned back, Steve had been joined by a woman who wasn't Lisa. Joined was maybe stretching it. The woman had come up next to him and turned in a hundred dollar bill for chips. She was a tiny little thing, just over five feet, but perfectly put together. Blond spiky hair looked great with her black rectangular glasses. Ben wasn't a fashion maven by any means, but he knew chic and trendy when he saw it. She had on this really tight white shirt that had no sleeves, but was a turtleneck, and blue cropped pants. The way she looked at Steve made it real clear why she'd stood right there. Then the woman, girl, whatever, looked at him, but only for a second. Her gaze moved to his left. Ben had to look. Next to him was another woman who looked to be the same age and type as the woman next to Steve.

She smiled at him with dazzling white teeth. No glasses, the same clear, pale skin. A brunette, she had squared off bangs and a blunt hair cut that reminded him of Theda Bara, the movie star from the twenties. Another beauty, and he wondered what they did for a living. He'd have said modeling, but Steve's gal was too short.

"You seem to know what you're doing," the brunette said to him. "I don't have a clue."

"That's a pretty good formula for losing your shirt."

Her smile took on a wicked gleam. "Maybe that wouldn't be so bad."

"Oh, my," Ben said. "I'll show you the little I know about craps, but as far as losing shirts or any other articles of clothing…"

"All right, fine. I'll play nice." She stuck out a manicured hand. "Melinda."

"I'm Ben. And this is my friend, Steve."

She reached across him, making sure to brush her breast across his shoulder. Her perfume was Obsession. "That's Gwinn, we're from L.A."

After the introductions were over, Ben placed his

bet, conservative, and sent a guarded look Steve's way. Steve wasn't looking back. He was deep in a conversation with Gwinn, who was eating up his every word.

Not at all like last night, when Steve had turned away the babe in the bar. This was more like watching the old Steve in action. God, he'd been a terror. Not that he was one of those dicks who go through women like tissues, but he'd always had his choice of the finest ladies. Ben had done real well, too, and he figured it was just overflow because he never did as well on his own.

But the truth was, Melinda, as beautiful as she was, had nothing he wanted. Taylor was somewhere in Las Vegas, and eventually, tonight, she'd be with him. Everything else was just hang time.

Steve laughed, loudly, then the waitress came by with their drinks. Melinda and Gwinn both ordered Bloody Marys.

"So what do you do?" Melinda asked.

He hated this part. Usually made up some wild story, but it seemed like too much trouble. "P.I. out of New York."

"P.I. as in Private Eye?"

He nodded. "And my buddy here owns a fleet of ships."

Her eyes widened as her gaze moved to Steve. Aha, a clue. Perhaps owning a fleet of ships made one automatically more attractive. Perhaps most people knew how being a private investigator was not necessarily the most direct method to millions. Go figure.

"No, like this."

Ben watched the maestro in action: Steve put his arms around Gwinn, bent her over the rail and helped her shake the dice before she threw. Totally unnecessary. Completely flirting. Undoubtedly trouble.

"Ben?"

He smiled at Melinda as she touched his shoulder. "Would you excuse me?" Then he turned to face a very perplexed Taylor Hanson.

TAYLOR COULDN'T BELIEVE how badly she wanted to slap the dark-haired bitch. But she simply smiled. Waiting to see how this little drama would play out. Her gaze moved over to her brother as he unwrapped his arms from the blonde. She'd never seen a darker blush on Steve's face. Not even when she'd walked in on him in his bedroom when he was fourteen and definitely "in flagrante."

"Taylor," he said. "Uh, hi."

"Hello, Steven. Your fiancé is in your room, lucky for you. But I'm quite certain she'd love to see you."

"Yeah, right." He gave a guilty smile to blondie, then after quickly scooping up his chips, dashed toward the elevator. The women gathered their meager winnings and skulked away, leaving her with Ben and a table full of anxious gamblers.

"Hang on," he said, stuffing chips in his pockets until he looked like a very successful thief. Then he put his arm around her and led her in the direction of the Pink Taco. "Did you have fun shopping?"

"It was heaven on earth. Who was that?"

"Her name was Melinda, and she was hitting on me."

"That much I gathered."

He smiled angelically. "She wasn't succeeding."

"I should hope not."

"A bit more worrisome about Steve, though. Last night, same scenario and he was true blue without a blink. Today, he was the old hound dog we've come to know and love."

"I don't get it. He's the one who's been so hot on Lisa. And you know what's funny? She was great today. Funny and nice and I was actually going to talk to you about forgetting this whole thing."

"I think, given this minor incident, the very least we should try is to get Steve to postpone, yes?"

She nodded, then looking away from Ben realized they were at the Nouveau Mexican restaurant. "What's this?"

"Food."

She looked at her watch. Four-fifteen. "Early, isn't it?"

He nodded. "I have plans later."

Her face heated, and she imagined she looked a great deal like her brother, only for very different reasons.

Ben leaned over and nipped her earlobe. "If I'm going to ravish you, I need sustenance. So do you."

A whole different shade of red must be making her face look clownlike and awful. "Food. Yes. Good."

"Unless you'd rather have something else. At the coffee shop perhaps?"

She thought about her fave Mexican dishes. All of them had beans. "Yes, actually. I would." She took his hand and led him back where they'd come from.

Then, instead of heading toward the café, she turned toward the elevator.

His brows rose in question.

"Room service," she said.

He pulled her to a stop next to a cashier's cage and put both hands on either side of her face. "Brilliant," he whispered. Then he kissed her, sucked her tongue straight into his mouth.

She nearly lost it right there. No more time to waste. Pulling back, she nipped his lower lip. "I don't want to be down here a moment longer."

"Yes, right." He grinned, then ran. Flat-out ran. With her running right behind him.

INSTEAD OF HER ROOM, they went to his. He'd insisted, although he wouldn't say why. As soon as they walked through the door, he put the Do Not Disturb sign out, then segued into the bathroom, closing the door behind him, and leaving her a bit in the lurch. But, as she'd seen quite often in the past few days, Ben was full of surprises, and that was much more fun than steady and predictable.

His room was virtually identical to her own, so there wasn't much to explore, but she did find the room service menu and gave that a quick peruse.

Before she could make up her mind, Ben was behind her, his hands on her hips, his lips on the back of her neck. "Did you miss me?" he whispered, his warm breath tickling in just the right way.

"Oh, were you gone? I hadn't noticed."

"God, you're cute. Mean, but cute."

She spun around, pleased that he didn't let go of

her. "It's true, you know. I am mean. But only when I don't get what I want."

His brown eyes steadied on hers. "What do you want, Taylor? What do you need?"

She grabbed him by the shirt and pulled him tight against her, answering with a searing kiss.

Ben rubbed against her, letting her feel his erection. He kept rubbing, pushing her backward until she was up against the wall.

They stood next to the wet bar, and she had a splendid view of the city out the window, although she had no eyes for anything but the man holding her wrists with both hands.

He yanked them up high on the wall and while she gasped he kicked her legs apart until her dress was tight and high on her thighs.

"Is this what you want?"

If she'd been able to speak she would have said yes, but his mouth was on hers, and she had to explain everything with her lips, her tongue, her body.

Kiss, then gone, then kiss, gone. Teasing, testing, grasping her wrists so tight that it would have hurt if she hadn't been so pumped full of adrenaline, among other things. "Stop," she said, but the word was cut off by his lips. A second later, he was gone again, just that brief taste, that quick lick with his darting tongue.

"Stay," she said.

He shook his head. Then he licked the underside of her arm, one long stroke, making her shiver and gasp. God, he was good at making her do that.

"Tell me what you want first," he said, that mercurial tongue of his rimming the shell of her ear.

"A kiss," she said. "A long one."

"No, try again."

"That's not fair."

"I never said it would be fair."

"You were in control last time."

"I like being in control."

"So do I."

"You like this, too."

She turned her head, knocking him on the chin. "Let me go and I'll show you how much you'll like being on the bottom."

"No."

"No?"

"Try again."

"Why should I?"

He smiled real slow. "Because I'm going to make you lose your mind."

"Too late."

He laughed. She watched his Adam's apple bob, and it was sexier than Elvis on Ed Sullivan.

She lifted her leg, snaking along the inside of his until her knee hit pay dirt. Not hard, of course, because she didn't want to hurt anything of value; just enough for him to understand that while he might have her hands captured, she wasn't without resources.

"Ahhh."

"So, where's my kiss?"

"You want to play rough, is that it?"

"Rough is good. Sometimes."

"Oh? How rough?" He nipped her lip again, this time making her cry out.

"Hey."

"Too rough?"

She smiled. "Am I bleeding?"

"No."

She didn't say anything else. Let him figure it out for himself. Ben was quite clever, and she didn't want to restrict his behavior in any way, although of course she reserved the right to say no if she felt like it. Today, feeling as wild as she did, he'd have to go pretty damn far for her to throw in the towel.

"You know what?" he said, just before he circled her lips with the tip of his tongue. "Foreplay is great. I mean it. Right up there with hot dogs at Dodger Stadium and swimming naked. But you know what's even better?"

She knew, but she shook her head anyway.

He held her up against the wall with his lower body, squared himself with her eyes and gave her the most commanding look she'd ever seen. "Do not move until I tell you to," he whispered, his voice somewhere between a promise and a threat.

She obeyed, holding still, holding her breath, almost stopping her heart, anticipating what was to come.

It became clearer as he released her wrists. Her instinct was to lower her arms, but his cocked brow stopped her dead still. It felt a bit silly to hold her hands up like that, but she didn't particularly care.

His hands moved on to much more useful tasks. Lifting her dress, for one. Slowly, the material rose, exposing more of her thigh, then the crotch of her panties, and still he kept lifting until he'd raised her dress past her chest, her head, her arms. He tossed it behind him, and she didn't give a damn where it landed. Next he reached behind her and undid the catch on her bra. That was discarded somewhere, and as he reached to do the same with her panties he bent his knees until his lips where level with her breasts, quite perky with her hands up in the air.

He kissed each nipple, then used his tongue to make her moan. She felt his fingers grab the edges of her silk thong and rip it away from her body.

There. She was naked right in front of him, standing up against the wall, once again with him fully dressed. She had to do something about this. Next time, dammit, she was going to strip him first, and not get herself into this situation.

Oh, who was she kidding? She didn't care one whit who got naked first as long as both of them ended up there.

Taking her by surprise, he lifted her straight up, his hands under her thighs. Her legs wrapped around him, and she'd been so busy being annoyed that he was dressed, she hadn't realized he'd actually lost his pants. Or maybe just lowered them. Whatever. Because what he did then stole her breath.

He lifted her onto himself.

Just. Like. That.

One second she was standing there, and the next he was inside her, fully, unbelievably. Her head rolled back as she cried out, as her hands flew down from the wall to hold on to him for dear life. She probably didn't have to, as he held her completely steady, but this wasn't exactly a position she was very practiced in, so dammit, she was hanging on.

Balancing her weight on the wall, he was able to pull almost all the way out, then thrust back in to the hilt. She gasped, cried, swooned as he entered her over and over, rubbing her in the most perfect way. Faster than she could have ever imagined, she felt the shiver and tightness that was the beginning of an orgasm. Maybe because so much was happening all at once, maybe because it was Ben and she could practically come just by looking at him, but holy cow, she was on the runway speeding toward takeoff.

"Oh, God," he said as he found her mouth.

The kiss was desperate, just like her own, and she guessed he was riding right next to her on the express to heaven.

"Jeeze, Taylor, what are you doing to me?"

"The same thing you're doing to me."

He buried his head in the crook of her shoulder, bit her flesh and kept on riding.

Then his face shifted to a grimace, but there was no pain involved. Just intensity that she knew too well. He cried out and their voices mingled as she peaked, her hands tearing at his hair, her feet banging on his back.

She had no idea how he was doing for at least a couple of minutes. Then she felt his strength wane as he struggled to regain his breath.

He let her down gently, and while she staggered to the bedroom, he followed close behind.

As she flopped on the gold comforter, she flashed on something uncomfortable. ''Uh, Ben?''

He grunted, which she took for a response. He'd flopped down next to her, and somewhere along the way he'd taken off his shirt and his pants, and was as naked as she was.

''We got a little carried away there, didn't we?''

He grunted again.

''Except that we didn't...I didn't...I'm on the pill, but that isn't...''

''I got it covered.''

''What?''

He lifted his head and looked at her. ''I had it covered. Literally. That's why I went to the bathroom first.''

''Oh. Good. But, just in case, I have a couple of condoms in my purse.''

His head flopped down on the pillow, his chuckle low and rueful. ''Wish I'd known that yesterday. Anyway, sleep now. Thank me later.''

''Okay,'' she said, but she sneaked in a kiss to his cheek anyway.

10

THE EARLY MORNING LIGHT hit Taylor right in the eyes. She turned over, but the damage was done—she was awake. Sore and awake.

Ben slept soundly, his breathing deep and even, his face unlined and perfect even with the dark shadow of beard. He was the most beautiful man she'd ever seen, and watching him made her heart ache. Odd, that tenderness could hurt so, but there it was. She was amazed at this man, at his thoughtfulness, his energy, his incredible sexuality. At the way he made her feel.

She closed her eyes, remembering the night, especially the second time they'd made love. He'd awakened her with a kiss, very gentle and sweet, and she'd opened her eyes to the sight of him leaning on one elbow, staring at her as if she were a thing of wonder.

"What time is it?" Her voice had been gruff with sleep, and Ben reached over her to the bedside table where he picked up the bottled water, gave her a sip, then put the bottle back.

"I don't know. Late."

"How long have you been awake?"

He shrugged his one free shoulder.

"And you've been watching me for how long?"

"As long as I could stand it."

"Excuse me?"

He laughed. "I'm not sure how long I've been staring, and then the temptation was too strong, and I had to kiss you. Even though I knew it wasn't a very nice thing to do."

"Kissing is always nice."

"But you looked so peaceful."

"I'll sleep again. Trust me." She rose until her lips found his. "Just remember, whenever the urge to kiss strikes, you have my permission."

His slow grin made her blush. "Does it matter where I have the urge to kiss you?"

She shook her head.

"Even if it's..." He threw back the covers and leaned over her chest, kissing the tip of her nipple.

She laughed. "Well, that probably wouldn't go over too well in say a restaurant or at the blackjack table."

He kissed her other nipple before coming back up to eye level. "Oh, sure. Just spoil it all, why don't you?"

She flung her arms around his neck and pulled him down. "Don't you go giving me any trouble, Ben Bowman."

"Or what?"

"Or things could get ugly."

He looked up at her. "No possible way. You and ugly don't mix."

She threw her arms back and spread her legs wide. "Take me. Take me now."

"Is that it? The secret to having my way with you? A compliment?"

"Not just any compliment, no. I mean, I probably won't lay down after you've said my chicken casserole is yummy."

"You sure about that?"

She shook her head.

He stroked her side as his head lowered to her neck. She felt his warm breath first, then the edges of his teeth as he nibbled. "I'll have to experiment with this. Try different kinds of compliments and see the various reactions."

"It won't work if I know you're trying to get some."

His head came up again. "I'm always gonna be trying to get some. Who do you think I am, for God's sake? A superhero?"

"There's trying, and then there's *trying*."

"Explain."

"If the compliment is heartfelt with no ulterior motives, then the points are quite high. If the compliment is heartfelt and you're groping me under the table, then the points lower proportionately."

"Lower, but don't get cancelled out."

"No. Not always."

"And what if the compliment is completely bogus, and I'm groping you right out in front of God and everyone?"

"Then there are absolutely no points whatsoever."

"And I don't get any?"

"Depends on how you're groping."

He grinned. "Interesting system you have there, Ms. Hanson."

"It's my playground, I get to set the rules."

"And the same goes for me, right? I get to set the rules?"

She blinked a few times, stared him straight in the eyes. "Are you trying to tell me that any form of compliment, heartfelt or otherwise, would have the least effect on your libido while I was in the process of groping you?"

"No. You're right. You grope, I'm yours. You could even call me names, say rude things about my goldfish, disparage my heritage, and if you're groping, there's no contest."

"The difference," she said, "between the sexes."

"Oh, there are lots more differences than that." His hand moved down her tummy until his fingers trailed through her soft curls to the folds of her sex. "See, you go in…" He demonstrated the principle using two fingers in just the right way. "…while I go out." He guided her hand to his very erect and insistent cock. "Big difference. Huge."

"I'll say," she said, giggling.

"See, now there's a compliment that works every time."

She pulled him closer. "Why don't you show me how this works?"

THAT HAD BEEN hours ago, when the night had been dark and the only light had come from the little lamp over the nightstand. She had no recollection of how it had been turned off, so exhausted had she been by their slow, incredible lovemaking.

He'd known exactly how to touch every inch of her, how to make her wait, how to build the tension, how to tease and definitely how to pay off. The truth was, he was everything she'd ever thought he was, and more.

She turned to face the wall, away from the sleeping man, no longer caring if the light hit her eyes. No longer caring about much but the building realization that she was in deep, deep trouble.

Everything she'd believed about Ben was true, and that wasn't good at all. She'd been so sure that she'd exaggerated his prowess over the years, that she'd built him into an icon of romance and sex in the fertile fields of her mind. She'd never really considered the possibility that he was the most incredible lover on the planet. The thought was ludicrous. No one could be as good as she remembered Ben.

Except Ben.

And where the hell did that leave her? How was she supposed to go on from here? Settle for boring sex for the rest of her life? Try every man she could find in the desperate hope she'd find someone as wonderful? Give up sex completely? She wasn't Catholic, but maybe being a nun wasn't such a bad idea. No, she'd have to be a lot more saintly, and a completely different person, so that was out.

She'd loved last night. Every single second of it. Now, as she tried to analyze why, her skin started tingling as she recalled his every touch. That wouldn't do.

Play the
Lucky
Hearts Game

and get...
2 FREE BOOKS
and a FREE MYSTERY GIFT...
YOURS to KEEP!

yes! I have scratched off the silver card. Please send me my *2 FREE BOOKS* and *FREE mystery GIFT*. I understand that I am under no obligation to purchase any books as explained on the back of this card.

Scratch Here!
then look below to see what your cards get you... 2 Free Books & a Free Mystery Gift!

350 HDL DZ55   150 HDL DZ6L

FIRST NAME   LAST NAME

ADDRESS

APT.#   CITY

STATE/PROV.   ZIP/POSTAL CODE   (H-B-05/04)

Twenty-one gets you
2 FREE BOOKS
and a **FREE MYSTERY GIFT!**

Twenty gets you
2 FREE BOOKS!

Nineteen gets you
1 FREE BOOK!

TRY AGAIN!

Instead she focused only on the facts, the empirical evidence. Why was he so much better than anyone else she'd been with? Better wasn't even the right word for it. Ben was to making love what the Mona Lisa was to art. Way the hell outside the box. But why?

She grabbed the almost empty water bottle from the side table and took a sip, wishing she had some coffee, but unwilling to wake Ben.

On the other hand, the water did nothing for her, barely even quenched her thirst. What she needed to do was get out of there, go somewhere alone to think. Somewhere she wouldn't feel Ben's heat next to her skin. Somewhere she didn't have the overwhelming urge to touch him and start the whole damn process over again.

Slipping out from between the covers, she began searching for her clothes, finding them more or less in the same area. She gathered them all and went into the bathroom. She'd shower in her room. Right now, all she wanted to do was make a clean getaway.

Once she was dressed and her hair would no longer scare anyone she met in the hallway, she opened the bathroom door. Listening hard, she waited a good minute until she was sure he was still asleep. Then she headed for the door. As her hand touched the knob, she realized she couldn't just sneak out without any kind of notice. That would be horrible and while she might not be worthy of nun status, she wasn't a complete rat.

She left the bedroom for the living room, and immediately found a piece of hotel stationary. Now, what on earth was she going to say?

No use overthinking the process. "Dear Ben, thank you for the most fabulous night. I've got a busy day ahead, so I snuck off to get it started. I'll catch up with you soon. Hope your dreams were sweet!"

She almost signed it, "Love, Taylor," but she didn't. He'd figure out it was from her, and then the "L" word wouldn't come into play.

The "L" word. No, no, no. She could not go there. She was in enough trouble as it was.

THE POOL WAS already crowded when she got there. Not as many kids as she'd have guessed, but then this was the Hard Rock, which wasn't really a kid-oriented hotel. But those that were there seemed to be having a really good time.

Mostly, though, there were a whole mess of beautiful women and handsome men, all of them wearing remarkably small bathing suits, some exposing more skin than she liked to show her doctor.

The expanse of flesh on display wasn't her concern at the moment. All she wanted was a quiet lounge chair, a cold beverage and time to write to her buddies while she decided whether she should shoot herself or not.

Because she clearly had wonderful luck when it came to pool chairs, she found a prime spot, spread her towel and made herself comfortable. Before she even had a chance to bemoan her fate once, a cocktail waitress came by. After several seconds of deep consideration, she ordered a Bloody Mary.

Soon enough she was left to her thoughts, and it wasn't pretty. She brought her computer to her lap and opened it up. She had enough battery power for a couple of hours. She couldn't log in, but that was okay because she'd downloaded her emails before she came to the pool.

She had just enough shade from a nearby umbrella to read comfortably. The first e-mail she opened was from Angel, one of the sharpest of the women in her Eve's Apple group.

To: Taylor
From: Angel
EveApple.com
Subject: Re: Arghhh!

Dear Taylor,

Sounds like you might be facing some trouble in paradise. Not that your plan wasn't wonderful, but if you're anything like me, the best laid plans have a way of turning into big, fat, hairy messes before you can say Viva Las Vegas.

So Ben is fantastico, eh? He sure sounds like it. Just don't get carried away, okay? Because from what you've said, this is one week of fun and games. One week. Not forever, not the rest of your life, not even the rest of the year. And, my girl, you have to go home and face the rest of your life, and um, sorry, but didn't you say that wouldn't include Ben?

Maybe I'm crazy, but if you can just look at this thing for what it is—great sex with a gorgeous man—and realize it's like Vegas itself, cool vacation, but not sustainable—then maybe you can nip the obsession in the bud, and just enjoy yourself! That's the point. Enjoyment. Pleasure. Bliss.

Also, in my experience, true supreme happiness with the opposite sex is meant to be temporary. Oh, yeah, they say it's forever in the books and the movies and stuff, but come on. We all know better. So isn't it more sensible to have one incredible, mind-blowing, world-rocking week than to go on forever wondering what could have been?

So you have to come back to reality. Face it, honey, we all do. Life isn't a fairy tale, but if you're lucky, you can be a princess at least for a little bit. And it sounds to me like you certainly have found your (short-term) prince. So enjoy. 'Til it's time to say goodbye.

Love, Angel

The cocktail waitress came with her drink, and Taylor had to mask the tears in her eyes with a hand up for shade, even though she was already under the umbrella. The sympathetic smile as she signed her tab signaled her failure at faking it.

"It's okay, honey," the waitress said. "Been there, done that. There's other fish in the sea."

"Thanks," she said, but all she really wanted was to be alone. To weep. Because she knew that while Angel's advice was right on the money, there wasn't a chance in hell she could take heed.

It was too late. Way too late. She'd gone back ten years, right back to the moment she'd first been with

Ben. To the magic that had been that weekend. To
the revelation that she would never, as long as she
lived, find anyone remotely as special or wonderful
as him.

Only this time, it was worse. Because she knew
what else was out there. And she knew there wasn't
going to be another man for her.

She went on to the next e-mail, this one from Kelly,
a biochemist from Seattle who also happened to have
been a model who'd graced the covers of *Seventeen,
Cosmo* and *Vogue*. Kelly was less hopeful than Angel,
which was a real pisser, because if someone as brilliant and beautiful as Kelly didn't believe in fate, or
true romance, what chance did Taylor have?

Depressed beyond measure, she shut the computer
and slid it under her chair. She sipped her drink, perfectly chilled and spicy, and watched the soap opera
all around her. Men flirting with women, women flirting with men; giggling, blushing, flaunting. She felt
as if she were watching the mating rituals of the flat-
bellied sun worshipper.

Everyone seemed hungry and desperate for a connection. The women laughed too brightly, the men
smiled with friendliness on their lips and lust in their
eyes. Arms were touched, shoulders brushed naked
torsos. It made her long for Ben's comforting presence, and horribly sad that what she'd found was so
fleeting.

Ben didn't want to get married. He'd made that
very clear. Steve had told her, twice no less, that Ben
had sworn to never marry again. Steve hadn't said
why, but she imagined it had a lot to do with his

divorce. She doubted very much he would be interested in living together. His attitude was closed and final, even though she knew he liked her a great deal.

She wasn't even sure she wanted marriage. The way she was drawn to him was unlike anything she'd ever experienced with anyone else. No one made her come alive like Ben, and no one sent her to the moon like he did. But even she wasn't foolish enough to think it was love. It was sex. Fantastic, fabulous, incredible sex. Nothing more. So why the big deal?

She had no idea. All she knew for sure was that she ached for him. She felt empty without him, and complete when he was near. What an idiot she was. It was too soon for feelings this intense. Way the hell too soon.

Just last week she'd been so excited about this unique opportunity. She'd bought clothes, makeup, underwear designed for seduction. She'd figured it would be a romp, but she'd also figured there would be a sad, but sweet ending.

Not this.

She took a long pull on her drink. At least she was familiar with what she would go back to. And it wasn't all bleak. She had her job, her friends, her motorcycle. And the utter conviction that she would never be truly happy.

Maybe that was too dramatic. Love wasn't only about fireworks. There were people she knew who weren't sexually active, yet they still had successful marriages. She'd find someone she could respect, someone who had a good sense of humor. There were good men out there, and now that she understood the score, she'd find herself one. Her expectations would be different, that's all. She'd had the best, now there would be the rest.

C'est la vie.

"Hi."

Taylor looked up, knowing the masculine voice above her wasn't Ben's. What she saw, on any other day, would have revved up her pulse. He was one hell of a good-looking man. Tall, blond, built like a champion athlete. His smile seemed warm, and he actually looked her in the eyes instead of letting his gaze roam. "Hi."

"I saw you sitting here alone. I was wondering if you wanted some company."

She didn't. But what the hell. Today was as good as any to start her new life. "Sure. Sit down."

He found a plastic chair and pulled it near her lounge. "I'm Cade Miller." He stuck out a long, tanned hand.

Her own felt dwarfed by his, and if this had been a week ago, she was sure she would have gotten all quivery at the touch. She forced a smile. "Taylor Hanson."

"I'm here from Utah," he said. "Spending a week in this crazy place with a couple of college friends."

"You're in college?"

"Not anymore. But we still hang out. I'm a pilot. I fly out of Salt Lake City."

"That sounds exciting."

"What about you, Taylor Hanson?"

"I'm a paralegal. From San Francisco."

"On vacation?"

She shook her head, took another drink. "Here for my brother's wedding."

"Oh, wow, that sounds like fun."

"I'm trying."

He scooted closer. "I know we've just met, but uh, are you okay? Is something wrong?"

She smiled again, meaning to tell him that now wasn't the best time. Instead, she burst into tears.

"Oh, God, Taylor." He looked around as if he'd been trapped with a crazy lady. Then he moved over to her lounge and put an awkward hand around her shoulders. "Don't cry, okay? Whatever it is, it's going to be all right."

"No it's not. I thought for sure I would get over him." She wiped her eyes with the back of her hands, but the tears kept coming. "It was a great plan, and it should have worked, but he's still Ben, and I still want him so much."

Cade patted her shoulder. "I'm sure he wants you, too."

"No, he doesn't."

"Then he's a fool. Because I can't imagine anyone not wanting you."

She looked through tears that blurred his expression, and still she could see the kindness in his eyes. "That's so sweet."

"It's true. You're very lovely."

"You probably think I'm nuts."

"Nope. I've had my share of moments. And you know what, they all passed."

"This won't."

"You don't know that."

She sniffed, and wiped her eyes once more. "Can I ask you a favor?"

"Sure."

"Kiss me?"

To his credit, Cade didn't run for the hills or call the pool police. "Are you sure?"

"Just once. Just so I can…"

He gave her a lopsided grin. Then he bent down, and took her lips with his.

BEN STOOD by the poolside bar, hands in his swim trunk pockets, watching as some blond Adonis kissed Taylor. He wanted to turn around and walk back into the hotel. It wasn't his business if she kissed another guy. They had no ties to each other. Just a week of sex and the rescue of her brother. It made no difference if Taylor wanted to sample the buffet instead of ordering from the menu.

On the other hand, Ben was pretty damn sure he could kill the guy without working up a sweat.

11

TAYLOR FELT his lips on hers, felt his hand tighten on her shoulder. But it didn't feel like it was her, doing this, kissing this stranger.

She pulled back, her cheeks heating with the flame of embarrassment. "I'm sorry," she said, barely hearing her own voice.

"For what?"

She couldn't look him in the eyes. "I'm a wreck, and you seem like a really nice guy. You don't need to be a player in my little psychodrama."

"Hey, if I can help..."

She smiled, meeting his gaze. "You can't. But thanks."

He turned his head slightly to the left. "Sure?"

She nodded. "There are so many gorgeous ladies here, all of whom would be delighted to meet someone like you. So go. Find fun. It's your vacation."

"I don't want to leave you like this."

She touched his warm, tanned hand. "I'm going swimming now. As many laps as I can without drowning. And then I'm going to sleep. So please, don't fret."

He sighed, looked around the pool, then back at her. "I think that's a pretty good idea. But listen, I'm in room 1202, so if you want to talk when you get up from your nap, don't even think twice.''

Glancing at his left hand, she saw no ring, not even a tan line where a ring would be. "How come you're single?"

He laughed. "Well, so much for small talk."

"I mean it. You're gorgeous, sweet, and unless you're a serial killer or still living with your mom, I don't get it."

He stared at nothing for a long moment. The outdoor speakers carried the sounds of Fleetwood Mac across the pool, and someone screeched in one of the private cabanas. When he looked at her again, her cheeks weren't burning anymore, which was good, although she really didn't want to think about actually kissing him.

"I haven't met her," he said.

"Her?"

"The one."

"Ah, but how do you know?"

"Because I haven't wanted to commit to someone. Not for the long-term, at least."

"So there have been almosts? Close, but no cigars?"

"Yep. And there's even been one that got away."

"Tell me about that one."

His smile turned rueful and his gaze moved from her eyes to somewhere around her ear. "She was amazing. I met her in Hong Kong. We were together for six days, and it was the most incredible experience of my life. We connected on every level. She utterly fascinated me, and I can't remember laughing so often and so hard.''

''What happened?''

''I had to fly back to the States.''

''Why didn't she go with you?''

''Because,'' he said, his voice dropping into the whisper zone, ''I didn't ask her. I'm not sure why, not even now. But I didn't. I did try to find her again, but she'd left the university there, and I have no idea where she ended up. I even hired a private investigator, but she dropped off the face of the earth. I've never really forgiven myself for that.''

''So, if you found her again, you'd want to keep her?''

''Only if she'd want to keep me.''

Taylor leaned forward and gave him a gentle kiss on the cheek. ''I'm sorry. I hope you find her.''

''And I hope you find what you're looking for.'' He stood up. ''I mean it about calling. I'll be here a couple more days.''

''Thanks.''

He nodded once, then headed toward the bar.

Taylor watched him until he'd ordered his drink, and then she got up. After putting her computer under her towel, she went to the deep end of the pool. There were swimmers and some kids playing with a beach ball, but she had room to maneuver. She dove in, the cool water shocking for only a second or two, then comfortable and safe.

She'd been a water child, and because of her, her parents had built a pool in their backyard. She never missed an excuse to swim, and she remembered many a late night, when everyone in the house was asleep, when she'd tiptoe out to the backyard, and in the dark, she'd take off all her clothes and dive into the cool black water.

She'd done a lot of thinking like that, stretching her mind while she stretched her muscles. Lap after lap, her body in a rhythm that made every part of her calm. Even today, her most sacred rituals involved the pool at her gym, although they frowned on skinny-dipping.

As she carved out her narrow route, she thought about what Cade had said. How he'd found *the one* and then let her go. Fear. He hadn't said the word, but that's what it was all about. Fear of commitment, fear of being trapped, of making a mistake.

Was she afraid? Of course. But of what? Losing Ben? Keeping Ben? Not having the guts to tell Ben the truth? Hell, even if she got past all that, Ben had his own fears. He'd been so adamant about not wanting to get married. It had rolled off his tongue as if he'd said it a thousand times.

She'd seen other couples meet and fall for each other. It looked so easy. As if they were two sides of the same coin; the key being that they immediately recognized that they were supposed to be together.

All she had with Ben was a shared past, the most incredible lovemaking in the world... She had to laugh at herself. She had been going to stop there, but that wasn't at all true. They had a lot more than that together. She loved his sense of humor, his intelligence, his probing nature. She loved the way he talked to strangers and the way he was with Steve.

Then there was his eclectic taste in music, art, books. The truth was, he was the most fascinating man she'd ever met.

She hit the end of the pool and dived under to start another lap. She'd stopped counting at eight and was just starting to feel the strain in her arms, legs and lungs. Five more, at least, and if she could bear it, eight more. She wanted exhaustion.

For two laps, all she did was focus on her body, on moving through the water. Then her thoughts went back to Ben.

It was ridiculous to call this anything more than what it was—a crush. That was it. Infatuation. Memories cascading with reality, making the connection electric and enticing as hell. But he wasn't the one. He couldn't be. He just represented what she wanted in the one. So what the hell did she want?

She didn't have a clue.

BEN'S EYES were on the football game, but his thoughts were out by the pool with Taylor. Watching her kiss another man. Watching another man kiss her.

He felt like crap. And aside from the too obvious ego blow, he wasn't quite certain why. Not that he didn't have every reason to feel bad—he'd made love to the woman for hours last night, and it had blown him into the next galaxy—but the depth of his despair was totally unexpected.

He liked Taylor, sure. More than he'd ever have guessed. She was a hell of a lot of fun, he had strong ties to her background, she made him feel like a total stud, not to mention how good he felt whenever he was with her, no matter what they were up to. Everything he could want in a friend with benefits. And damn, those benefits were beyond world class. But come on. It wasn't as if she'd left him after two years of marriage. For another woman. This was a no-strings attached week, and all he could think about were strings and more strings.

So what was up with that?

Okay, so it was back to his ego. He had to admit, it hurt. Wounded him deeply. Man, he'd thought she'd had a blast last night. If that was faking it, the woman deserved an Oscar, a Tony and an Emmy.

No. No one was that good. He'd watched her face, her body. Seen her physical reaction with his own two eyes. Had felt the contractions when she'd come, and no matter how much moaning a woman does, there was no way to fake that. She'd come, and come hard.

So why would she need to play kissy-face with that jerk?

He signaled the waitress, and she came over wearing a big smile and a skimpy outfit. He probably should have done something about her welcoming grin, but instead he ordered a gin and tonic. She winked at him as she moved on to the next customer.

Hey, there was proof. He wasn't a total dog. In fact, experience had told him that women seemed to like his odd looks. Taylor had always acted as if she thought he was pretty hot stuff. She hadn't hidden her sexual agenda at all.

So, if he were investigating this situation for a man checking up on his wife, what would he deduce?

First, that the client had better watch out because

something wasn't right. Women who are happy don't stray. Women who are getting it the way they want it don't look elsewhere.

Second, he'd look beyond the obvious. He'd been standing across the pool from the couple in question, unable to read their lips or even read their expressions with any degree of accuracy. Maybe he'd misinterpreted the scenario. Perhaps the guy was an old friend, someone she hadn't expected to run into. Or he could have been an old boyfriend. That would have explained the intimacy.

Almost.

That hadn't been a buddy kiss. Not for tan-boy at least, and Ben hadn't been able to see Taylor that well. That kiss had intent, and the position of his body and his hand around her back confirmed it. However, Taylor could have intended the kiss to be friendly and nothing more, and the jackass had taken advantage of the situation.

Ben hadn't seen her hands. She could have been pushing him away the whole time. And he hadn't stuck around to see the aftermath of the kiss. Big mistake. If it had been a case, he deserved to be fired.

But it wasn't a case, it was Taylor. His anger had eased, but his ego still ached like a wounded puppy. What seemed clear was that there were other explanations for the incident. He'd never go to a client with such flimsy evidence.

The right thing to do was to find out more. Just ask her. Tell her he was down at the pool, and he happened to see her with her friend. Her reaction would tell him everything, and then they could have a laugh over the whole thing. Or not.

But he still would ask. Because he didn't want to keep feeling this way. Not for another minute.

TAYLOR CARRIED HER TOWEL underneath her arm, covering her computer. Damp beneath her cover up, she had accomplished her goal. She was exhausted all the way to her toes. Physically and mentally. All she had to do was make it to the elevator and down a short hall, and she'd be home free.

But, because she was Taylor and life wasn't in the least bit fair, she never made it to the elevator. Her brother stopped her halfway there.

Not that he saw her. She saw him. And what she saw made her stop.

Steve stood alone, leaning against a cashier's cage. He had a glass of clear liquid in one hand, and his other hand was cupped, holding what she guessed were pills. When he threw them in his mouth and drank down the water after, she figured she had it right.

What was Steve doing taking pills? He didn't even take vitamins. The man was sickeningly healthy, worked out daily, ate like an athlete in training. And he had a thing about aspirin. She'd never seen him take one. Not for a hangover, not for the flu, not even for a broken wrist. He'd always been that way, and nothing and no one was going to change his mind.

He scanned the immediate area with a guilty look, then headed toward the Pink Taco. She wasn't about to let him get away. Hurrying, maneuvering through too many vacationers and gamblers, it took her several minutes to get within shouting distance but she finally caught him by the back of his shirt.

He spun around so sharply she gasped, and then he recognized her, causing the mask of anger to drop from his face. Slowly, he formed a sort of smile. "Hey."

"Hey. What are you doing?"

"Me?" He shrugged. Stared at the towel under her arm. "Hanging. Lisa's getting a massage. I've been wandering."

"Oh."

"What about you?"

She looked down at her damp cover-up. "Swimming."

"Cool. Well, I think Lisa's probably done so—"

"Not so fast, mister."

His lips tightened.

"What were you doing back there?"

"Where?"

She pointed back to the cashier's cage. "Right there. I saw you."

"You saw what?"

"You. Taking pills."

"So?" The word sounded simple enough, but the flush on his cheeks said something different.

"So, you don't take pills."

"I do now."

"What kind?"

"Vitamins."

"Bullshit."

"Hey," he said, as if wounded by the crude word. "Anyway, it's none of your damn business."

"It is so. You're my brother."

"And you're not my keeper."

She could tell from his body language that she'd hit a mighty big nerve. Steve wasn't like this to her. To anyone, really. It wasn't that he didn't have his secrets, but he was always nice to her about not sharing. Always. "Come on. You're starting to scare me now."

"Don't be scared. There's no reason."

"Then tell me the truth."

He shifted to his left, but she grabbed his arm. He stopped, looked her in the eyes. "Don't."

"I care about you."

"I know."

She didn't let him go. Not with her heart pounding and her senses on high alert. "Will you tell me one thing?"

"It depends."

"Does Lisa know?"

"About me taking vitamins?"

She nodded, knowing they weren't talking about vitamins at all.

"Yeah, she does."

Taylor sighed. She really couldn't press anymore. He was a grown man. An idiot, but fully grown. Something was wrong, and it was a sure bet that it had everything to do with this quickie wedding. Her first instinct was to go to her mother, but she didn't want her to worry. So she'd go to Ben.

Ben would help her. He'd find out what was going on here. And she had to see him anyway.

She let go of her brother, but not before giving him a kiss on the cheek. "Go on. Find your Lisa. Just don't forget you've got a bunch of folks who care about you, okay? And we're all here, whenever you need us."

Steve's posture changed, relaxed a little, but she could see he wasn't thrilled about the conversation. He squeezed her hand. "I remember."

"See you later."

He nodded, then walked away from her. She stared after him until she lost him, then turned back to her own path. She should sleep, just for a bit. Then she'd face Ben and tell him about the pills. She wouldn't tell him about the rest of her morning, though. Not about the way she felt. Not about what she wanted. Because she didn't know.

12

BEN CLOSED HIS EYES on the way up to the fourteenth floor. The elevator wasn't too crowded, just two teenagers checking themselves out in the mirror, giving him the occasional glance, hence the closed eyes. He didn't want to smile or act nice. He wanted to figure out what the hell was going on with him and Taylor. He wanted to sleep. He didn't know what the hell he wanted.

The doors opened, and he walked out. There, standing in front of the second elevator, was Taylor. She noticed him with a start.

"Hi."

"Hi."

They both just stood there, staring at one another, until both elevators closed and went on their way. They were alone in the carpeted hallway, and he could cut the tension with a knife. This wasn't how he'd pictured seeing her again. Hell, he'd expected to see her next to him in bed. The note had been simple but terse, and his suspicions had been aroused. Then to see her at the pool... The night had been one of the best of his life, and then he'd gone down the rabbit hole into some parallel universe where Taylor was with some strange blond guy and he didn't know what to say.

"I was just, uh…" She nodded in the direction of their rooms.

"Me, too."

"Great." She started walking first, and he followed, slightly behind her. He could see the tension in her posture, the way her bathing suit was still damp so her white cover-up clung enticingly to her behind. Despite his concern over what happened, his libido seemed to be in fine working order. His gaze traveled down to her bare legs, slightly tan, perfectly formed, and he wanted to run his tongue down her thighs to taste the chlorine and what lay beneath. He was so engrossed in his trip down erotic lane, that he almost bumped into her when she stopped at her room.

He did something to her because her towel dropped to the carpet with a clunk. A clunk? Then he saw her laptop peeking from beneath the terry cloth.

He bent to get it, and when he rose again, he noticed the blush on her cheeks. He hadn't said anything about wanting to lick her thighs, had he? No. This was about something else. And he had a damn good idea what.

He held out the computer and towel. And before he could stop himself, he blurted out, "So, who was he?"

Her eyes widened and her mouth opened. The blush deepened and went right down to her neck.

He silently cursed himself. That wasn't the way he'd planned to bring the whole thing up. And now she was on the defensive, which was the exact opposite reaction he'd been going for. Damn, damn, damn.

"Who?"

He blinked. Who? Was she kidding? "The guy at the pool." Hell, he'd gone this far already, no use backtracking now.

"Oh, yeah." She turned to the door, struggled with her key card. "You want to come in?"

"Sure," he said, although the thought of running away held great appeal.

TAYLOR FINALLY got the door open, and led him inside the room. He'd seen her kiss Cade. Oh, God. Of all the things she hadn't prepared for, that was the biggie. Her cheeks were aflame, she didn't know where to look, her hands shook, and all she wanted was to blink like Jeannie and disappear into a bottle. Any bottle. Instead, she dumped her towel and computer on the couch and made the quickest getaway she could. "Let me go change. I'm still wet. I'll be back in a minute." She inched her way to the bedroom. "Get something from the minibar. Or room service. Or whatever. I won't be long. I—" Then she was inside the bedroom and she shut the door.

She leaned against the door, cursing her bad luck, her stupidity, her lack of magical disappearing skills. He'd seen her!

She had to tell him something. Anything. Heading to the closet, she picked out a summer dress, this one sea-foam green, with wisps of pale blue that she'd gotten on sale at Nordstrom's for a steal. To add to her luck, she'd found perfectly matching sandals at a completely different store, days apart. It seemed obvious she'd reached her luck quota with this dress, so she'd be damned if she didn't wear it until it shredded.

Next, she got a pair of panties from her drawer, blue, to go with the dress. Not that anyone was going to see her color coordination, as Ben would now discover that she was a blatant slut that didn't deserve anything but his pity.

She went into the bathroom and took off her clothes, stepped into the shower to rinse off the chlorine and tried to come up with a lie.

Any lie.

Okay, she could say that Cade was someone she knew from San Francisco. Just a friend. A pal. A buddy. No one important or sexual. And the kiss? Ha, ha. That was just a friendly hi. No big deal. So how about them Yankees?

She scrubbed her skin with the hotel soap, hand-milled and smelling like lemons. So if not a buddy, then what? An ex-boyfriend? So why would she kiss an old boyfriend? Because he was dying, that's why.

Yeah, Cade looked like a guy on his last legs. *Come on, girl. You can do better than this.*

He couldn't be a dying ex. But the friend thing wasn't too bad. Lots of friends kiss. They don't usually use tongue, but how close would Ben have had to be to see Cade's tongue in her mouth.

The friend thing would work. It would. As long as she told him in a completely casual fashion. No drama. No blushing! Of course, she was well known for her terrible lying skills. Her boss had caught on quite early, and made sure she was never in any kind of position where she had to so much as fib.

Besides, lying to Ben felt like hell. Worse. He didn't deserve it. All he'd been was wonderful and truthful. And last night was one of the most glorious nights of her life. How did she repay him? By kissing a stranger at the pool the next morning.

Maybe slut was too kind. What was worse than a slut? She didn't want to know, although she was sure that's what she was.

God, Ben. Wonderful Ben, who had the audacity to turn her little fantasy into a world of confusion.

She rinsed off, stepped out and got dry in a flash. Her hair, which she should have washed, she simply left in the ponytail. So what if it was wet. As for makeup? Forget it. He deserved to see her for who she truly was. She wasn't good enough for mascara.

On with her panties, then the dress. Damn, but it was a great dress. Perfect lines, silky material, and it really made her look tan. Which wasn't the point. The point was Ben. Waiting. Deserving so much more than her.

She slipped on her shoes, straightened her back and headed out for the lie-fest in the living room.

BEN CLOSED the minibar door. Opened it again. Nothing new tempted him. He slammed it shut, making the whole shelf tremble. Cute trick of hers to disappear like that. She had plenty of time to work out a believable alibi, and here he was wandering around like a schmuck, waiting. He should go.

He walked to the door. Opened it. Shut it. This was

Taylor, for God's sake. She wouldn't lie to him. Why would she need to? They'd made love. So what? So it was the best he'd ever experienced in his life, but hadn't that been the deal? A week of hoppin' and boppin' and adios, amigo. So what if she had a little tongue action out at the pool. This was Las Vegas! Sin City! He could be getting a lap dance right this second, if he wanted one.

But that was just it. He didn't want one. He didn't have the slightest desire to kiss another woman. He wanted Taylor. More of her. Lots more. And right this second, he was terribly afraid the fun was over.

What had he done wrong? Everything had seemed so right. Almost too right. Like that made sense.

The bedroom door opened, and he froze, as if she'd caught him going through her purse or something. He struggled for a smile, but the struggle was short-lived as he watched her walk into the sitting room.

She was a vision in a pale green dress. Fresh-faced, her hair back in a simple ponytail, completely unadorned, and looking so beautiful it made him want to drop to his knees and beg for forgiveness. He didn't give a damn that he had no idea what he should be forgiven for. He just wanted her.

His gaze moved down over the curves of her breast to the incline of her waist. Then the flair of her hips did something to his groin that wasn't exactly on the agenda.

"Sorry," she said. "I just hate that feeling of chlorine after swimming."

He nodded, although he couldn't remember the last time he'd been in a public pool. He liked water, but not that much of it. "You're probably tired," he said. "I should get going. Maybe grab some lunch or something."

"No, it's okay. I, uh, you asked about…"

He shook his head as he walked toward her. "Forget it. It's none of my business. Man, you look so beautiful in that. It's a knockout."

She smiled, the first genuine expression except for fear and guilt he'd seen today. "Thank you."

He looked down at his jeans and his vintage Island shirt. It was covered with pineapples and old Chevys for some unknown reason, but he loved the damn thing. Didn't get a chance to wear it often. Next to Taylor, he felt like a little match boy.

He stepped closer to her, wanting to touch her, maybe her arm, her shoulder, before he left. Maybe get a hint of her scent to carry with him.

She touched his arm instead. "Ben, listen."

He hated sentences that started that way. He put his hand up to stop her, but she didn't even notice.

"That guy at the pool? He wasn't anybody. I mean, he was a really nice guy. Sweet. Cute. And he came over to, I don't know, try to pick me up or something."

"You don't have to tell me this."

"Believe me," she said. "I hadn't planned to. Now, I think I have to."

He nodded, not sure he wanted to hear the rest. But if she needed to talk, he'd listen.

"I was really confused about a lot of things. And he was just there. And when he leaned over—"

Ben coughed. That thing about listening if she

needed to talk? Bullshit. No way. "Hey, you know what? I really am hungrier than I thought." Walking backward, he prayed he was heading for the door. "I'm gonna go get one of those famous foot-long hot dogs. On the Strip. I saw a whole show about them on the Food Channel. They're supposed to be great."

"Wait."

"Really hungry."

She took a step toward him. "It's about Steve."

He stopped. This he could hear. "What about him?"

"I saw him down in the casino. And he took some pills."

"Pills? Steve?"

She nodded, concern all over her gorgeous face.

"That's weird. What were they?"

"He wouldn't tell me. Actually he said they were vitamins."

"That's a load of crap."

"Which is what I told him."

"And?"

She turned toward the window, to the brilliant sunshine just outside. The searing heat that was just a mirage inside the cool hotel room. "He wouldn't give it up. Although I asked him if Lisa knew he was taking vitamins, and he said yes."

"Vitamins."

"I think it has something to do with all this."

"Knowing his pill-phobia, I have to concur. It doesn't look good."

"I don't want to say anything to Mom. She'd just get worried, and I'm doing that for both of us."

He walked over to her side, put a hand around her shoulder. It was easier now, because he was talking to Steve's baby sister. Who needed his help. "I'll find out what's going on."

"He's not going to be thrilled I told you."

"I'd be shocked if he didn't expect it. For God's sake, we're his family."

"I know. I said that to him. But you know how stubborn he can be."

"Yeah, ask him who got to sleep in the big tent four summers in a row."

"Huh?"

"Never mind. Just know, I'll get to him. Before the wedding."

She faced him now, just Taylor. No swimming-pool men, no embarrassed blushes. His Taylor. "Thank you."

He kissed her then. Those sweet peach lips. The soft honey of her breath. Her scent, unique in all the world. He kissed her and wanted nothing more than to be around her. To feel her skin from time to time. To hear her voice.

"I gotta go," he said, not wanting the moment to be spoiled. "But I'll call you later, okay? See what you're up to?"

"I'd like that a lot," she said.

He believed her. It was enough.

"But I want to—"

He put his lips back on hers, then inched away to whisper, "Shh. Later."

And because he'd been very, very good, she kissed him back. Kissed him like she was his and his alone.

BEN WALKED past Caesar's Palace, marveling at the statues and the huge sign for the Celine Dion show. She must be raking it in. He heard it was one of the better shows on the Strip. He'd wanted to see O, too. But he didn't think he'd have time. Maybe he could catch something, a comedian or a magic show. He'd like to take Taylor to see Lance Burton. That was one he'd seen before, and it was a trip.

But he didn't see the sign for the giant hot dogs, and besides, he wasn't really that hungry. He was definitely hot, though.

He stepped inside a small casino, one he didn't recognize. It was cooler by a whole hell of a lot, and for that he was grateful. But it was loud. Really loud.

In some of the bigger hotels, they made sure the slot machines were demure, hushed. In here, it was every bell and whistle they could find to drum up business.

He wandered, his gaze moving from one gambler to the next, their faces blurring into one another. He walked all the way toward the reception desk area where the noise abated to a manageable level.

There, a big red couch sat unencumbered and inviting, so he sat down, sinking into the leather cushion. He took his time looking about. The two people behind the desk, a man and a woman both wearing red blazers with nametags, seemed older than the folks employed at the bigger hotels. He was glad they had work. And that they were laughing.

Across the way was one of those old-fashioned shoeshine stands, but there was no attendant. And besides, he was wearing tennis shoes. A bellman studied his manicure, leaning against his podium. That was the total action, and Ben was most grateful.

He reached down to his belt and lifted his cell phone from the holster, flipped it open and used speed dial. He wasn't sure why he was calling Alyson, but he didn't hang up. She answered after four rings.

"Hey, it's me."

"Hi," she said. "I thought you were on vacation."

"I am. I'm in Vegas, ostensibly looking for a giant hot dog and a cheap beer."

"You must be thrilled."

"Actually, I'm having a pretty good time. Except I'm not sure Steve should be getting married."

"You don't think anyone should get married."

He sighed. "Why did we?"

She didn't say anything for a while. "Are you sure you didn't already locate that cheap beer?"

"No, Alyson, I'm sober as a judge. And I need your help. Why is it we got married?"

"Because we loved each other."

"We did, didn't we?"

"Yes. And in a lot of ways, I think we still do."

"Just not that way."

She chuckled. "No. But you're still one of my best friends."

"Yeah. I know."

"So why are you asking me this? Existential angst? The nearness of someone in love?"

"Both. Neither. I'm here with Taylor. Steve's sister."

"Right, you've mentioned her."

"She used to have a really big crush on me."

"And?"

"I think it might still be there."

"Oh."

"And I think I might have one on her."

"Oh!"

"Yeah. But I'm not sure. About anything."

"Tell you what, Benny. Do me a favor. Give it a minute. Stick with the confusion. I know you hate it, but before there can be any good decisions, confusion has to be dealt with. So don't run."

"I can't run. I'm the best man."

"Good. And here's something else. Do not, let me repeat, do not, let my sexual orientation be your excuse. I'll hate you if you do that."

"I won't."

"Promise?"

"Yeah."

After another long silence where he thought he'd lost her, he heard a gentle sigh. "You're one of the good guys, Ben. As scared as you are of all this love business, I can't think of anyone on earth who deserves it more than you. You're good in love, sweetie. If it hadn't been for, you know, I wouldn't have let you go for all the tea in China. So hang in there."

He smiled, appreciating the white lie. "You sure this whole lesbian thing isn't just a phase?"

She laughed. "I gotta go. Be good. I love you."

"You, too. And, thanks."

He clicked off the connection and settled back into the soft sofa. Love? It wasn't that serious. God, no. Like? Sure. Lust? Oh, yeah. But not love. He wasn't about to go there with Taylor or anyone.

He simply hadn't realized a person in lust could get so jealous.

13

TAYLOR WOKE UP disoriented, unsure whether it was day or night or where she was. Unfortunately, that lasted only a second or two, then she realized she was in the hotel and that Ben had been utterly present in her fitful dreams.

It had been a long time since her emotions had been this rattled. Years. Not that she didn't have the most normal of lives, with work problems and victories, friends who were all too human, men issues. But it occurred to her that she'd actually designed her life to have very few real problems.

She sat up, pushing the big pillows against the headboard. She didn't turn on the light. The dark was better suited to this line of thought.

Staring into the dim room, she focused instead on the patterns of her adult life, and what she saw was as startling as Ben's cheekbones. She really had built herself a nice little safe nest.

Her job challenged her, but in the end, she wasn't responsible for the individual cases. Someone else, the attorneys she worked for, had their heads on the chopping block. She did research mostly, typed up legal briefs, ran errands. She lived within her means, not getting herself into trouble there, but also not risking anything to get ahead.

Her friends, and she had a comfortable group, weren't the kind she'd had in high school. Back then, it was all about heart-to-heart talks, intimate confessions, deep discoveries. She played poker with these guys, went to movies and plays. Talked about sex.

The closest thing she had to real intimacy was in her Eve's Apple online group, people she'd never seen in the flesh. And all she had to do to bow out of that gang was stop answering.

Sobered and unsettled, she clicked on the bedside lamp. The light made her wince, but it wasn't half as jarring as the glaring illumination on her life.

Come to think of it, Cade had been a perfect example of who she'd become. Nice guy, good-looking, not threatening in the least, but she hadn't been interested at all. If Ben hadn't been in the picture, she might have gone for drinks with him, had a few laughs. Who knows, she might have had vacation sex. But she would have done all that because he didn't live in her neck of the woods. Because he was a vacation guy. Because it meant she didn't have to get involved.

A chill passed through her and she brought the covers up to her chin. Oh, God. What if she had this whole thing with Ben all wrong? What if she'd used him, all these years, as an excuse? Sure, the sex had been great, but was that really it? Or was he just convenient? So she didn't have to think, or risk, or try. Not once, in all those years had she put herself on the line. She'd never loved anyone. She'd never even let herself get close.

And now that Ben was back, were her feelings for him real? Did she even know him? More importantly, did she know herself? What did she really want from him? Ten more years of excuses? Or were her feelings for him genuine, and he hadn't been an excuse at all, but a reason.

She glanced at the clock on the nightstand. In two hours she had to be down in the lobby to meet the wedding party for the fancy dinner Lisa's mother was throwing. Picasso's. Elegant and expensive as hell, she had to look great.

Throwing back the covers, she padded to the bathroom. She'd brought some wonderful lavender bath beads with her, and a mud mask for her face. At the same time, she would do a deep conditioning treatment on her hair, and she might even have time to change her nail polish.

But just after she turned on the water in the big bathtub, she went into the living room and got the small radio from the shelf. Taking it into the bath, she put it on the sink and found a radio station that played the oldies. She didn't want to think.

"HEY, STEVE. Call me. We've got some time to kill before dinner, so let's kill it with a vengeance, what do you say? I'm on my cell."

Ben hung up, wondering if Steve really was busy or if he was avoiding him. He'd undoubtedly assumed Taylor had shared about the pill incident. Steve taking pills. The only thing that would sort of make sense was if the pills were Viagra, but that didn't seem likely. To the best of his knowledge Steve had never had problems in that area, but what the hell did Ben know?

He didn't know squat. About himself, about his life, about Taylor. He was a man who was all about digging into other people's lives and avoiding his own.

It was time to leave the soft comfort of the red couch. Hours had passed as he'd observed the comings and goings of the people at this little hotel/ casino. Older folks, mainly, but mixed in with kids he would have carded in a heartbeat. He'd made up lives for many of them, certain that he was miles off the mark, but he didn't care. It was a way to pass the time. A way to stop thinking.

But always, he'd come back to Taylor, and he couldn't make up a life for her, even though he desperately wanted to force her into a safe, comfortable cubbyhole, easily dismissed when he went back to the real world.

Something had happened to him last night. Something he couldn't explain. When he'd been inside her, he'd felt…different.

Damn, he wasn't good at soul searching. Mostly, he was good at bullshit, but what she'd done to him wasn't that. Not even close. She'd made him feel things he hadn't felt before. New territory. He hated new territory.

What it meant, he had no idea. That he cared for her? Yeah, that much was true. He did care. But what the hell did that mean?

He liked how he was with her. The whole time sitting here, some part of him had wished she'd been next to him. He wanted to talk about all the people he saw, share his observations, and more perplexing, hear hers.

Him. The loner. Who preferred dinner solo, who liked the quiet of his apartment, with his fish his only obligation.

Even when he'd been with Alyson, he'd never had this strong a desire for her company. In fact, what made them work as long as they had was their separate lives. They got together, sure, but mostly for the odd dinner, and of course, the bedroom. The demands there had been minimal, and only lately had he admitted that it hadn't bothered him near enough.

Alyson had been more of a buddy than a wife, and when she'd left, he'd been upset, sure, but also relieved. That was the real truth, wasn't it? He'd been glad to have a place to himself. Accountable to no one.

Maybe that's what had attracted him to her in the first place. He could have the comfort of a steady woman, without any of the real work a relationship required.

What did that say about him? That he was a selfish son of a bitch? Well, yeah, that was a given. But there was more. He felt it, he just couldn't pin it down.

And why was he worrying about it now? What was it about being with Taylor that had him questioning his motives, his lifestyle?

He walked into the casino and headed right for a video poker machine. Fishing out a twenty, he played for a while, hitting a pretty good jackpot, four fours with a kicker, early on, so he didn't have to think about much. He just stared at the cards as they came up. He made it a game to see how fast he could hit the buttons without screwing up. The machine took him away, and that's just where he wanted to be. Away.

But not forever. Because between the aces and the kings, there was Taylor. Beckoning. The scent of her hair, the look in those astonishing blue eyes. She pulled at him, tugged at his heart with her gentle laughter.

By the time he was back down to his original twenty, it was late. He only had forty minutes to get back to the hotel, get dressed and meet everyone for dinner.

Whatever else was going to happen, tonight would be interesting. He had no idea what he was going to say to Taylor. Only that he wanted to see her. And he needed to get Steve alone, too.

He cashed out, letting the quarters drop into the white plastic bucket. He'd catch a cab to the hotel. They had to get dressed up tonight. Crap.

THE ROOM REEKED of class and money. And gorgeous art. Picassos dotted the walls, real ones. Of course, the restaurant was Picasso's at Bellagio, one of the most elegant venues in all of Las Vegas. Taylor could see it was going to be an experience to remember.

She tore her gaze away from Ben to check out the details of the place, but it wasn't easy. He'd worn this gorgeous dark suit, slim slacks and perfect one-button jacket. Underneath was a slate-gray, distressed silk shirt with a matching matte silk tie. The man was to die for, and every woman they'd passed had proved it.

But, she really did want to look around. The room was huge, although somehow it also managed to feel intimate. The floor-to-ceiling windows with incredible gossamer drapes framed the water show in front of the Bellagio. The dancing fountains were amazing, and she'd made it a point to walk by at least once every visit. Tonight, no matter where they sat, they'd get an unbelievable view. Inside was just as spectacular. On the muted walls were displayed a collection of Picasso's original artwork. She'd seen prints of some of his etchings and paintings but they paled before the spectacular power of the originals.

They were taken to their large table in the back by a smartly attired maitre' d, who wasn't, thank goodness, in the least condescending or snooty. In fact, he looked like someone she'd like to play cards with.

Ben pulled her seat out for her, and when she got in position, he discretely sniffed her neck. Oddly, it was an incredibly erotic moment, and she got a little swept away, but Lisa's mother brought her back into the room, pronto.

"We thought it would be nice to go for the prix fixe menu, although if you want you can get the degustation menu, which is, of course, more of a tasting thing, but I hear it's wonderful. And if no one minds, I'd like the sommelier to help with the wines. Go ahead and order cocktails, though. It's going to be a long evening, so we might as well live it up. Daddy's paying for all this, so the sky's the limit, isn't that right, sweetheart?''

Lisa, who looked beautiful in a classy black dress that showed off her figure and also showed off the exquisite gold necklace around her neck, laughed along with her mom.

Poor dad. She already knew the meal was going to be way up in the hundreds. Oh, well. Steve seemed happy. Kind of.

He kept losing his smile. One second he'd seem joyful and thrilled to be right where he was, and the next second the happiness would simply melt away and he'd be blank. Not morose, not angry. Just nothing. But that never lasted. Whenever Lisa spoke to him or glanced his way, the smile came right back.

Pauline, seated between her and Steve, seemed slightly bemused by the whole evening. Not that she hadn't been to fancy restaurants in her time. Her mother traveled, especially when she'd been younger. Taylor suspected her distraction was due to her concern about Steve.

Ben had been the picture of attention since they'd met at the Hard Rock lobby. It was as if this afternoon had never happened. He greeted her with a sizzling, if short, kiss, and had been wonderfully attentive and complimentary. He really did seem to like her dress. It was another Michael Kors, which she never could have afforded if it hadn't been at a resale shop. The python print felt daring, and the fact that it was basically a tube dress that hit her about midthigh, helped, too. She'd gone with leather pumps in dark gray to match the dress, five inch heels, no less. Being so tall, she'd worn her hair unadorned so it fell straight down her back. And she'd brought her little purse, the one that wasn't so much a purse as a leather baggie.

The waiter came by with menus, and it took them all a moment to ohh and ahh, but finally, they decided to go with the prix fixe. Which meant they had choices. Taylor started with the warm quail salad with sautéed artichokes and pine nuts. Ben had the poached oysters.

And then it was cocktail time, and she went for a straightforward martini. So did Ben. She smiled as he finished his request, and when he turned to her, his gaze locked on hers. Her entire body responded. Not just her breath catching, which it did, but her head felt lighter, her eyes as if the rest of the room had dimmed. Her breasts tightened, her tummy did, too. As for what was happening below the waist, she didn't dare dwell on that. She had a whole, long dinner to get through.

"You are the most beautiful woman I've ever seen," Ben said, his voice just above a whisper and completely private. "I can't believe I get to sit with you, talk with you."

She blushed, even while she acknowledged how over the top the words were. She felt the same way. That she was privileged to be with him, that the way he looked at her was a gift.

She leaned closer to him, so her lips were near his ear. "I just want to get something cleared up before we're busy with dinner and wedding plans."

He smiled.

"I'd like to do that thing again tonight."

"That thing?"

She nodded. "You know. That thing we did last night?"

"Oh," he said. "*That* thing."

"Yeah."

He turned so their lips almost met, but didn't. "I'm pretty sure that could be arranged."

"Good."

"Not yet. But it will be."

She placed her hand gently on his thigh. The muscle twitched beneath her palm. "You do know you're driving me crazy, right?"

"Ditto."

"Excellent. I didn't want to be the only one."

"Hey," Steve said, butting right in. "You guys do that hanky-panky junk later. Tonight's for my girl. She's our star, right?"

Lisa lit up. Her sparkling white teeth practically glowed in the candlelight. She kissed Steve on the cheek. "You're such a mensch."

Taylor and Ben burst out laughing. The word, coming from Lisa, was so unexpected and, well, crazy. It actually took them a while to calm down. But she took it like a champ.

"I'm not from another century," she said. "Just another state."

"Sorry," Ben said. He held up his martini, which had been delivered so smoothly, Taylor hadn't even noticed. "To Lisa and Steve. May she continue to surprise you. May he continue to be the same guy we all know and love."

Steve looked at Ben sharply, then toasted along with everyone else. Lisa just looked happy. Her mother had some large mixed cocktail, something red, which she drank pretty quickly while the rest of the party sipped.

"Hey, Steve," Ben said.

The bread course had come to the table and Taylor couldn't wait to try it. It smelled like heaven, and she made no pretense about the fact that she was starving.

"Remember that time that guy from Texas hooked the scuba diver?"

Steve cracked up, and there was something a little different about this laughter. It was the real Steve now, the guy she'd grown up with.

"Oh, man, was he pissed, or what? That Texas dude played him for what, half an hour?"

"Yeah, screaming the whole time, 'It's a whale! It's a whale!'"

Taylor laughed although she'd heard the story a dozen times before. But what she really liked was the idea of reminding Steve about his love for what he did, and what he'd be giving up if he moved to Kansas. "Remember that pregnant woman who caught that huge yellowtail, and she went into labor?"

Steve moaned, leaned back in his chair. "She wouldn't stop. She was screaming, and bending over double. Man, she was huge. But she wouldn't let go of that damn rod. She kept it up for like forty minutes, I swear. Caught the damn fish, and almost had the baby on the deck."

"She had it in the ambulance, didn't she?"

Steve, laughing, nodded. "Damndest thing I ever

saw. And her husband sent me a picture, after? Of the fish!''

They went on like that, Steve and Ben swapping tales, funny, silly, outrageous, and Taylor just leaned back and enjoyed the ride. A glance from her mother told her that she approved of the conversation, too, but not so with Lisa. At first, she laughed, smiled, went along with it all, but after the first course arrived and the boys went on and on, Taylor could see she was getting prickly.

It wasn't fair, but this was serious stuff. Steve without his boats was like a race car driver without a license. He wouldn't be Steve.

She probably should have stopped it, but she didn't. Instead, she ate the most delectable food in the universe. Tiny portions, but oh, God, the most succulent, fantastic flavors. The bread was crispy on the outside and soft and perfect inside. Ben swooned over his oysters, which started another whole round of fishing tales. It wasn't until they'd been served the second course that Lisa had had enough. She stood up, gave Ben a truly hateful look and excused herself.

Taylor felt like the heel she was. She followed Lisa to the bathroom, but when she went over to talk to her, all she got was chipper chitchat. Nothing real. But the evening would have to take another turn, or things would get ugly.

Maybe Ben could catch Steve alone tomorrow. Talk to him. Find out about the pills. About everything. In the meantime, she intended to enjoy the hell out of the rest of her meal, including the sumptuous wine and heavenly sounding desserts. Then she was going to take Ben to her room, and ravish him until he couldn't walk.

No more thinking. No more worrying. Back to the basic plan. Fun. Wildness. Sex and sex and sex. Eventually, she'd figure it out. But she wasn't about to waste what could very well be the last truly incredible fling of her life.

14

THE WHOLE WAY in the taxi back to the Hard Rock, Taylor and Ben had only touched hands. That's all. But what touching it was.

All of Taylor's erogenous zones were on maximum alert, and she felt even the slightest brush of his finger everywhere at once. Mostly in her chest, which had forgotten how to breathe properly, and in her sex, where she finally understood the concept of being in heat. Big time.

She could hardly look at him. Not that he wasn't amazing to look at, but when she did, sitting in that gorgeous suit, his hair mussed and touchable, his eyes smoky and filled with wicked promises, she wanted to yank down her tube dress right there in the back of the Yellow Cab and attack him.

It was only a few blocks to the hotel, she could wait. Or at least she hoped she could.

His thumb rubbed against her wrist, the thin skin feeling nearly as sensitive as her clitoris. At that thought, she had to shift in the seat, cross her legs and squeeze them together.

His legs were crossed, too, with his thigh covering his fly. She guessed he was having a difficult time of it, given that the two of them sounded like they were in the middle of a ten-mile hike up a steep mountain.

The taxi pulled into the parking lot of the hotel, and it took a frustrating five minutes to get to the front door. Ben had the fare and tip ready, and then the doorman helped her out of her side. Ben met her at the curb, put his arm around her shoulder and hustled her inside. When they got into the casino, he sneaked a glance her way, and they went even faster.

She couldn't help herself, she started giggling in the elevator. There were three other people on board, and one young couple kept their hands on each other's fannies. The single man kept looking at Taylor's chest. She found it unbearably funny, and trying to stifle the laughter made things worse.

Ben turned completely around, but she saw his shoulders shake. Too much juice running through them, she knew, but it didn't help. Something had to give.

Once they were on fourteen, they practically ran down the hall. She got the door open in one swipe, and then they were kissing, and his hands were all over her, and she was peeling back his jacket so she could get him naked, and everything was hot and moist and desperate.

His tongue explored her, plunged into her, dueled with hers. His teeth nipped sharply, and then she sucked deeply, getting him right where she wanted him. The devil pulled back, panting. "Wait," he said.

"Why?"

He smiled. "Get into your bikini. I'll be back in two minutes."

Before she could get the first word of her protest out, he was gone, and she was left breathless by the door, her purse somewhere on the floor, her body shaking with a desire only he could inspire.

Swimming? Now? She wished he would have stopped and told her what he had in mind. She didn't need to get wet. She already was.

But because she was the horniest woman in Nevada, she went to her bedroom and changed in record time. The bikini was the new one she'd bought shopping with Lisa—black and tiny, although it wasn't a thong. She wouldn't wear one of those in public, not for anything. Although when she looked in the mirror, she wasn't going to win any modesty awards. Her boobs looked much bigger than they actually were, her hips seemed curvier and even after the divine meal, her tummy didn't look half-bad. It was the tan, of course. She'd snuck some time in the booth back home before coming out here, just to lay a base. Yeah, she knew it was bad for her, but oh, man, it made everything look so much better.

Which wasn't the issue at the moment. She grabbed her cover-up and slipped on her flip-flops, and she was ready to go. Except for her purse. But she didn't really need one, if Ben would carry her key.

She found the little dinner bag and took out what she needed, then stood by the door. Not for long. He rapped twice and she let him in.

He wore black and dark green trunks, a funky Hawaiian shirt, and dark sandals. He'd pushed his hair back with his fingers, and he looked so good she could eat him with a spoon.

"Come on," he said, holding out his hand.

"Why are we doing this?"

"Because I need to expend a little energy."

"I have a really good way for you to do that," she said. "Right here."

"And I will, I promise. But later. This first."

She took his hand and let him lead her down the hall. "Hold this for me?"

He took her key and put it in his shirt pocket. Then he kissed the back of her hand.

"Are you sure?"

He nodded. "Yeah. I want to take things down a notch before we start up again. And, I want to play with you in the pool."

"Marco Polo?"

"Find the salami."

She laughed out loud just as the elevator door opened. They got in, and they were alone. Ben maneuvered her back against the wall, and he pushed up flat against her. "You look hot in that."

"It's just a cover-up."

"You look hot in everything."

"Ha. You should see me in my old chenille bathrobe at home. I look like someone's grandma."

"Kiss me, Granny," he said, but he didn't give her much of a vote. His lips came down on hers and once again, she lit up like a lightbulb.

Her hands moved down the smooth material of his shirt. He toyed with the hem of her wrap, and then she felt his fingers at the waistband of her bikini.

"What are you doing?" she whispered.

"Exploring." His fingers moved underneath the material until she felt him in her curls.

"Stop. They have cameras in here. I saw it on TV."

"They can't see anything," he said. "I'm blocking you."

"But they'll know."

"Then they'll be jealous," he said. "Let 'em. You're mine tonight. All mine."

Her head went back with a mixture of a giggle and a gasp as his finger slipped inside her.

"What's this?" he asked. "We're not even at the pool, and you're all wet?"

She pushed against his groin. "And what's this swelling? Allergic to something, are we?"

"I do believe the opposite is true. I thrive inside you, Taylor. I come alive."

"Oh, my," she said, just before they hit the casino level.

He pulled away in the nick of time, but she knew she was blushing like a fool. His cheeks were pretty damn pink, too. He grabbed her and led her to the nearest pool exit.

Once they were outside, they laughed again, and Ben loved the sound of it. She was like a kid. In fact, like the kid he remembered her to be. She'd been such a little pest back then, but he'd gotten a real kick out of her stubbornness.

Oh, who was he kidding. She'd worshipped him since the time they'd met, and that hero worship had turned into a major crush, and that hadn't all gone in one direction. Taylor had been an important part of his growing up years. Easy to talk to, when she hadn't been bratty, and interesting in her own right. He remembered seeing her in a dumb school play. It hadn't been a big part, but she'd knocked the hell out of it, and gotten the biggest ovation of the night. She'd glowed. Loved the attention.

And then there was the night she'd asked him to teach her to slow dance. She was going to the junior prom, and she didn't know how to do the slow kind. Her dad wasn't around, and Steve was pretty much a goofus, so he'd stepped up to bat. Not that he was any Fred Astaire, but it had been nice. Sweet. That night he'd realized she had a crush on him. He'd been flattered. And when, two years later, she'd invited herself into his bed, there was no chance in hell he'd say no.

Which didn't mean he wasn't still confused as hell. That kiss this morning, her odd half explanation, his reaction. Way more than he wanted to think about, especially tonight. Tonight, they were going back a step. To what they did extraordinarily well together.

But first, he wanted to feel that body rub up against him in the pool. He wanted to see her shimmer under the water. He wanted to strip her naked and make love to her, but he figured he could contain himself until they went back up to the room. Then they'd have the pleasure of a hot shower, drying each other off. Then howling at the moon as they turned each other inside out.

Chris Isaac was singing about a bad bad thing, making Ben like the hotel more and more. The fact that the pool wasn't all that crowded helped, too. Just a couple of late swimmers, the usual crowd around the swim-up bar, and the cabanas. That's where he led Taylor.

The first three were full, but the fourth had a lone guy, looking a little long in the tooth. "You here by yourself?" Ben asked.

"Evidently."

"Bummer."

The guy sighed. Ben recognized the sound of a man who'd been stood up.

"There's a whole gaggle of gorgeous babes by the bar."

"Yeah, but not the one I wanted."

Ben placed Taylor just outside the cabana wall. "Hold on." Then he went in and sat next to Mr. Lonely. "Listen, I'm sorry your thing didn't work out. And it's rotten of me to even ask, but I'd surely love to bring my lady back up here after a swim." He reached into his pocket, behind the two room keys, where he'd stashed a couple of hundred dollars. He took one bill out and slid it across the table. "Why don't you get a drink, and when we get back, you could go in and try your luck again."

The guy stared at the bill for a long time, then raised his gaze to Ben's. "Yeah, sure. Why the hell not?" He took the money in his fist. "Maybe I'll win something huge and she'd find me a little more interesting."

"You never know, brother. You never know."

"You want me to order something for the two of you?"

Ben grinned. "You're all right. Sure. A piña colada for her, a scotch on the rocks for me."

The stranger gave him a lopsided grin. "Go on. Get out of here before I change my mind."

Ben stood, clapped the guy on the shoulder. "Excellent karma points, my friend." Then he took Taylor's towel from her hand, waited until she'd given him her cover-up, gulped as he got a load of her in her black bikini, and stripped down to his own trunks. He left their stuff on an empty chair, gave a thumbs-up to his new best friend and followed Taylor to the edge of the pool.

She dove in first, and he followed a few seconds later. He found her leg, her calf to be precise, and hung on until they both came up, sputtering. She dipped her head back, letting her hair smooth from her face, and he did the same. They were at the deep end, so they had to tread water to keep their heads up. He got close enough to touch her everywhere he could.

"It's so beautiful here at night," she said, her gaze moving from the lighted palm trees to the colored lights placed directly in the water. "Like paradise."

"Have you ever been to Hawaii?"

She nodded. "I love it there."

"Me, too. I know a little private beach. We could make love in the sand."

"Ouch."

"True. But there are ways."

"I'll bet," she said, and then she kissed him. Her lips were moist and cool, but inside was the same wet heat he'd already memorized. He loved the feel of her smooth teeth, the way she tasted. He could dine on her forever.

The kiss deepened and then they were both coughing. Making out while treading water wasn't cutting it, so they swam far enough for their feet to touch. Another couple, not too far away, had the same idea, and they were at it hot and heavy. Ben couldn't have cared less. All he could see was Taylor, and the way she glistened in the moonlight.

She ran her hands over his chest until she found his nipple. He jerked when she squeezed him there, but came back for more. His hands were on her back, moving slowly down the length of her. When he hit her bikini bottom, he kept on going until he held the firm globes of her buttocks in each hand.

"Didn't you used to hate swimming?" she asked him.

"Me?"

"Yeah. Steve told me something about that a long time ago. That you could have been a really hot jock on the swim team, but you said you didn't like the water."

"I don't know how hot a jock I could have been, but it's not the water I dislike. It's the whole team thing."

"Then what the heck are we doing here, when we could be in private?"

"I said I don't like team sports. There's no one here but you and me, as far as I'm concerned, and honey, you in the water isn't something I was willing to miss."

She swung around, turning them both as she

wrapped her legs around his waist. "What are you talking about?"

"I got this image in my head. This morning, to tell you the truth. And I couldn't shake it. So I took you down here."

Her whole body kind of deflated.

"Hey, don't go there. I told you. I don't care what happened."

"But I do."

"Why?"

She had her arms around his neck, and he balanced her easily in his hands. She fit like she was made for him. Her head went back for a minute and he simply stared at her neck. So beautiful. He wanted to spend a week licking and nibbling that long column.

Her head came down and she looked him in the eyes. "I'm going to tell you something, and you have to shut up and listen."

"Okay."

"I had an entire plan worked out for this week," she said. "Aside from the wedding."

He grinned. "I figured it out."

"No, you didn't. I mean, you figured out what I was after, but not why."

He wasn't real sure he wanted to hear this.

"You do remember our weekend together?"

He laughed out loud. "You could say that, yes."

"Well, I do, too. I remember it too well. And it's kind of…screwed me up."

"What do you mean?"

She put her legs down, unwound her arms. He didn't want to let her go, but he did anyway. She didn't get far. "That was the most amazing weekend I've ever had," she said, her voice much lower, and younger, somehow. As if she'd gone back to that time ten years before. "You were my first, and frankly, my best."

The bang of her words hit him right in the ego and he felt his chest rise with peacock pride. That lasted all of about five seconds. "And that's a problem?"

"Yes, that's a problem. Come on, Ben. It's been ten years. And what we did that weekend has totally blown everything since off the map. How fair is that?"

She sounded affronted. Indignant. He couldn't help his burst of laughter. She responded by hitting him in the arm.

"Hey," he said, rubbing the pain. "That hurt."

"Well, don't laugh at me."

"I'm not laughing. I'm bewildered. Confused. Not laughing."

"What's so hard to understand? You spoiled it for me, Ben Bowman. Every guy I met after you failed the Ben Test. I mean it, there just wasn't…"

"Wasn't?"

"I don't know. The magic. Whatever."

"Whatever," he repeated. "And your plan was?"

She sighed, as if he was particularly slow. "To have a repeat performance, so that I could get rid of all the crazy ideas I had about you. About us. So that I could bring you down to size. Get a real life."

"Oh."

"What are you all disappointed about?"

"I'm supposed to be happy that I'm not your number one stud muffin?"

"What are you talking about? What do you think the whole problem is? Are you dense?"

He held back a grin. Damn, but she was beautiful when she was completely irrational. "Evidently."

She slugged him again, this time on the chest. And this time, her hand stayed right there, her fingers warm against his cool skin. "Damn it, Ben, it failed. The whole plan. Utterly. That's why I kissed Cade."

"Want to run that by me again?"

"I was confused, because of our night. Because it was even better than I remembered. Because, oh God, now I'm really in trouble, and how in hell am I supposed to get on with my life when I know that when I'm with you, it's like…"

"Magic," he whispered.

She nodded, looking like her heart had been broken into tiny pieces. "I kissed him because I should have liked it. He's like this great-looking guy. And nice. Totally buff."

"But?"

"It was nothing. Worse than nothing. A joke."

"Am I supposed to be sorry?"

"I don't know." She walked a few slow steps away. "I don't know much of anything, except I'm completely bewildered by the whole thing. You were supposed to be just a guy. A regular guy."

"And I'm not?"

She turned around. "Not to me."

15

BEN WENT UNDER WATER, and stayed there for a while. The lack of oxygen was an excellent distraction from the thoughts bombarding his brain. She was upset that he was good in bed? That she'd never had anyone better than him? Maybe he hadn't understood properly. Women had always confused him, and this was just another example of how they were from a different planet. Right?

A hand grabbed his hair and pulled him straight up. Right back into Taylor's face.

"Drowning isn't going to get you out of this, mister."

"I don't know. It seemed like a pretty good option."

"Ben, cut it out."

He folded Taylor into his arms. "I'm sorry, hon. I don't mean to be treating this...thing...lightly. I'm just—"

"Confused. Welcome to my world."

They stood for a while, moving gently back and forth in the warm water. He closed his eyes, letting himself enjoy the feeling of her body against his, so much of her naked. Smooth. Slick.

"I shouldn't have said anything," she whispered.

"Yeah, you should have."

"But now both of us don't know what to do."

He pulled back far enough to look at her. "You're wrong. I know just what to do." He kissed her, gently at first. After her lips parted, he entered her, moving slowly and precisely, in no rush at all.

Her body relaxed into his embrace as she shared the kiss. Music, something by Vanessa Williams, wafted through the palm trees and the water, and somewhere out there he heard laughter. But he didn't want to be out there. Not even an inch away from this warm woman, this incredible woman. He had to wonder, albeit briefly, if his overwhelming reaction to her touch had anything to do with what she'd just told him.

Probably not. He'd reacted this way ever since that weekend, long ago. Since she'd first showed up on his parents' doorstep. When he'd made love to her then, it had been the most shattering thing he'd ever experienced. Until this week.

Damn. No wonder he was having so much trouble with all this. He hadn't put it together, that's all. Being with Taylor was completely different from being with anyone else in his life. Everything was completely different, and if his life depended on saying how, he'd be a goner. It just was.

But it was also just sex. Great sex. Incredible sex. Nothing more. So why sweat it? He had her, here, in his arms. They had a cabana. They had a room. It would be moronic not to do what they both wanted.

He pulled back from her lips and moved slowly down to the side of her neck. She moaned, and he figured they better get out soon, because he didn't want to have any spontaneous emissions here in the very public waters of the Hard Rock pool.

"Come on," he said, turning so his arm was around her shoulder and he was leading her to the steps. "There's a drink waiting for you topside."

"Oh, good," she said. "Get me drunk so I don't have to think anymore, okay?"

He laughed. "It's not the end of the world, Taylor."

"Not yours."

"Not yours, either. We'll figure it out."

She didn't say more as they climbed the steps and headed for the cabana. The guy was still there, but the moment he saw them, he picked up his drink, sitting next to theirs, nodded a sad goodbye and went on his way.

Once they were alone, Ben handed Taylor her towel as he dried himself off. It was far more interesting to watch her than to pay attention to damp spots.

God, she was the most beautiful creature on earth. Her skin was as smooth as satin, and her curves were the essence of what was magnificent about women.

Unfortunately, his little—or should he say big— problem wasn't going anywhere, so he found his seat and put the towel over his lap. It was important not to focus on Taylor at the moment. He'd be much better off thinking of say, Joe Panzer, the thug he'd been tracking back in New York.

Only, Joe was far away, and Taylor was bending

over really, really close. He could see the curve of her breasts, and he was lost.

He took hold of her shoulders and brought her down on his lap. "I can't get enough of you," he said.

"Yes you can. You have to. We're leaving in two days."

"I don't want to think about that."

"Me, neither. But I can't help it."

He nibbled her earlobe. "Hey, let's just leap off that bridge when we come to it, okay? This is our vacation, and we're the lucky ones. Did you see that guy who just left? He's so jealous of us he could spit."

"I know. And believe me, I'm happy."

"That doesn't look like a happy face."

Instead of the smile he expected, he got an actual frown.

"What?"

She quirked her head slightly to the left. "Tell me about your day."

"Uh, I woke up without you—"

"I don't mean today. I mean your normal, average day."

"Oh." He really didn't want to talk about his life, but he also didn't want Taylor to move. Every time she moved, even a little bit, she rubbed him just enough to make him go a wee bit crazier. "It's not very exciting."

"Tell me."

"And there really isn't an average day."

She yanked on his hair. Not hard, but enough to smart.

"Ow."

She didn't say another word. But then, she didn't have to.

"Fine. I get up. Normally around six-thirty or so. But it depends."

"On?"

"Whatever I'm working on. If I'm tailing someone who's a night owl, then I have to be a night owl, and I sleep during the day. If I'm doing white-collar investigations, I do the nine-to-five thing."

She settled down, doing that wicked thing with her butt. "That's better."

"I'll say," he whispered.

"Hmm?"

"Nothing. Okay. I have coffee. I like coffee. I grind it myself. It has no vanilla or hazelnut or chocolate in it. It's just coffee. Strong."

"Uh-huh."

"And sometimes I have breakfast."

"Not always?"

"Not if it's nine at night."

"But you try to eat healthy?"

He turned his head for a second. "I try."

She grabbed his chin so he was facing her. "How often do you succeed?"

"At least once a week, I eat something green. That isn't mold."

She sighed. "Okay. Continue."

He closed his eyes and pressed his chin against her bare shoulder. "I work out six days a week. There's a gym two blocks from my place. Nothing fancy, just weights. And I run.''

''At the gym?''

''Around.''

''Tell me about your place. Is it an apartment?''

''A co-op.''

''Big?''

''For Manhattan? Huge. For anywhere else? No.''

''Do you have a bedroom?''

''And a small office. Really small. But it holds my computer stuff.''

''Go on.''

''Actually, I like where I live. I've got a great king-size bed that I spent a fortune on. I can't afford to be down with a bad back, or not sleep well.''

''A comforter?''

He nodded. ''Navy blue.''

''Good sheets?''

He shrugged. ''Sheets.''

''Hmm.''

He looked up to meet her troubled gaze. ''Sheets are a chick thing.''

''Not after you've slept in Egyptian cotton.''

''You want the rest?''

She grinned.

''I have a decent TV. I get cable. I like watching the Sci-Fi Channel. And Discovery.''

''No Playboy Channel?''

''Sometimes.''

''Your living room furniture.''

''I've found some decent pieces. I like old wooden

furniture. And leather. I have one of the top-ten great couches.''

"What about the kitchen?''

"Great coffeemaker. Excellent knives and pots. I don't cook much, but when I do, I don't screw around.''

"Last question about the co-op, I swear,'' she said, crossing her heart. "What about art?''

"Art?'' He was a little distracted by where she'd crossed herself. Real close to the edge of her bikini top.

"On the walls?''

"Oh. Yeah. Nothing fancy. Some stuff I've accumulated over the years. Things that I like.''

"Anything I'd recognize?''

"Probably not. I tend to go to small art shows, flea markets, that kind of thing. No posters by Erte or Van Gogh prints.''

"I see.''

"So, do I pass?''

"Oh, yes.''

"Phew.''

She laughed. "You couldn't have failed, you goose.''

"So is it my turn?''

"Yes, I suppose it is.''

"Okay. What do you want?''

She stilled. Completely. Not the reaction he was hoping for, but he supposed she had expected him to ask about her furnishings. He didn't give a damn about those. He wanted to know what all this meant.

"Tell you what," he said. "Why don't you reach over and get our drinks while you're thinking."

"Great idea." She uncurled her arm from around his neck and reached for the drinks, but she could only reach his. She ended up getting off his lap, and he stole the moment to do something he should have done when they entered the cabana. He closed the curtains. Then he sat down again. This time, he didn't use the towel, although if she looked, she'd see that despite the conversation, his hormones were fully engaged.

Handing him his drink, she took a long sip of her piña colada, and then she climbed on top of his lap again. Once they were settled, he drank, then put the glass down on the floor next to him.

He liked the cabana this way. A little on the dark side, but the candles on the table illuminated them both enough to see what was important. She still pondered his question while he went back to studying the rise and fall of her chest.

"One hell of a question there, Ace."

"I know. But I still want an answer."

"So do I."

"What do you mean?"

She sighed, resting her head on his. "I don't know what I want. Except that I want more of this. What I have with you."

"Are you saying you want to continue this after we leave Vegas?"

"Yes. Maybe." She squeezed his shoulder. "I don't know. All I'm sure about is that my plan went to hell in a hand basket. And now…"

"Now you have to face some things that maybe you didn't want to?"

She nodded.

"Like maybe you weren't rejecting those guys because they weren't great in the sack?"

Her head jerked upright, and she looked at him accusingly. "What?"

"I'm just guessing here, but something tells me this whole thing isn't just about sex."

"It is so."

"Oh?"

She stood and walked over to the other chair, all the way across the table from him.

"Look," he said. "I don't mean to upset you. You're the one that decided you liked this truth business."

"I told you the truth. It is about sex."

"Okay. If you say so."

"Dammit, Ben. It can't be about more than sex."

"Why not?"

As she sat, she picked up her towel and covered herself. "'Cause I don't want it to be."

"Ah, good answer."

"Stop it."

He went over to her side, knelt by the chair and took her hand in his. "Listen, Taylor, I think you're an incredible woman. I can't imagine any man in his right mind not thinking you're incredible. The odd thing here is that you haven't found one that you find just as great."

"It's not that easy."

"No. It isn't. And it's a lot harder when you have a built-in defense mechanism at the ready."

"Who died and made you so smart?"

He laughed. "It's a lot easier to see from over here, that's all."

"So what's your story? Why aren't you blissfully happy with a wife and two kids?"

"Tried it."

"And she was gay. Right. So what about after her?"

He shook his head. "Haven't had a lot of interest."

"In women?"

"In a relationship."

She leaned over, resting her chin on his head. "Oh, Ben, don't you dare tell me you think she went gay because of you. That's not possible."

"I don't think that."

"Good."

"But I also know that her being gay wasn't all that was wrong with our marriage."

She sat back. "Oh?"

He stood up. Not so much because he wanted to get away, but because he was getting a cramp. He walked over and got his drink. "We were always more friends than lovers. We had separate lives. Separate interests. It was like having a roommate, not a wife."

"Do you think that's why you married her?"

"More than likely. And to be honest, if she hadn't decided she wanted a real marriage, I wouldn't have complained. I was happy with things the way were."

"Oh."

He shrugged. Took a drink. Felt the burn all the way down. Thought about telling her the darker truth that came after the marriage ended. About his doubts, his fears. But she didn't need to hear all that garbage. "I'm not a complicated man, Taylor. I like things simple. And I try like hell to be honest with myself. I'm not the kind for marriage and all that. I'm good at looking at other people's lives. Not my own."

She didn't say anything. For so long, he went back to his chair, sat down. Drank some more. Wondered if he should have kept his big mouth shut.

Then she stood, so abruptly, he almost dropped his glass. "Let's go to my room," she said. "Okay?" She put her drink down, slipped on her cover-up. "Let's just forget all this and do what we do best." She stood over him. "Please, Ben. Let's just go."

He wasn't about to argue.

BEN TOOK THE SOAP from the little dish on the side of the shower and rubbed it between his hands until he'd built up a fistful of suds. Then he smiled as he sidled up real close to her, with the water hitting her back. He began at her neck. His slightly cooler hands, slick with lemon-scented bubbles, rubbed her slowly, tenderly. She let her head fall back, closed her eyes and let him take her to another world.

The combination of the water sluicing down from the crown of her head, his body rubbing against hers, and the divine feel of his soaped hands massaging her flesh was almost too much to take. She had to steady herself with her hand against the shower wall, especially when he moved down to her chest. She'd had massages before, but no one had ever done this. No feeling had ever come close.

His touch was intimate, reverent. Just below the slippery soap was a hint of coarseness, of masculinity, that was echoed in the sheer size of him. He circled her skin, taking his sweet time, slowing even farther when he got to her breasts.

One hand caressed each globe. Round and round, but not touching her nipples. Her very erect, taut nipples that were aching for equal time.

She almost stepped to the side to force the issue, but she didn't. There was too much pleasure in the tension.

He moaned, and she pushed her chest out, knowing he couldn't wait, either. His palms cupped her, and the touch, light as the bubbles of soap themselves, made the world spin. Nipples were great, wonderful, but no one had told her they could do *this*.

"Oh, God," he whispered.

All she could do was nod. Just the one time, because she was so damned unsteady on her feet.

His hands moved down her body, killing her with disappointment, thrilling her with anticipation.

She was drowning in bliss as he touched her, rubbed her, anointed her with his healing strokes. As his hands shifted below her waist, he stepped closer, rubbing himself against her belly. His fingers trailed down through her curls until he slipped inside her slippery folds.

As he circled her clit with the pad of his finger, he captured her lips in a kiss that made all other kisses fade. His tongue, like quicksilver, darted, thrust, retreated, tasting everything, leaving her breathless. Her hand went from the wall to the back of his neck as she steadied herself and him while she gave as good as she got.

He never let up with his fingers, teasing her mercilessly. Her muscles tensed from her calves to her thighs, all the way to the back of her neck. She was going to come, soon. It wasn't fair. She should have soaped her own hands, returned the magnificent favor he'd given her. She vowed to do that the second she could focus on something besides the orgasm that shut out the rest of the universe.

Her head fell back with her cry, her hands grasped his neck, his shoulder, squeezing as the wave built and climbed and brought her to her toes.

Somewhere out there she heard his low chuckle, but the bastard didn't let up, even though she was so sensitive the pleasure bordered on pain. But then, the hint of discomfort fled with an onslaught of ecstasy that lifted her beyond anything she'd known. She yelled out so loudly, she drowned out the shower, but she didn't care. Nothing mattered but the sensations, the bliss, the man.

He brought her down gently, as if she were a wild creature who needed to be tamed. His hands, still slick, petted her sides, her hips. His body bolstered her, kept her upright. And then he kissed her.

She opened her eyes, finding he'd done the same. Seeing his gaze, she moved back, even though she didn't want to break the kiss. More important though, was to see him. To be amazed at the emotions so clear on his face.

His hand moved to her cheek. "You're crying."

She wiped her eyes, knowing the moisture hadn't been from the water behind her. "I didn't know."

"I'm hoping they're happy tears."

She laughed. "I think that's a pretty good assumption. My God, Ben. That was…"

"I'm glad."

"But you."

"What about me?"

"I just take and take. It's not fair."

He stepped back. Glanced down. It took Taylor a second to realize that he wasn't rock-hard any more. "You?"

He nodded. "It's all your fault. You're so amazing, I couldn't hold back another second."

"Wow."

He grinned. "I'll say."

"I'm going to need a moment or two here, just to catch my breath, but then, Ben Bowman, it's my turn. You are going to get in my bed, and you're not going to move until I say you can."

"Oh, really?"

She grabbed his hands and swung them around his back. Of course he could have broken her hold in a second, but he didn't. "Really."

BEN GRIPPED THE SHEETS and tried to remember how to breathe. In fact, he was stunned the sight in front of him hadn't stopped his heart. Taylor, crouched over his body, slowly lowering herself onto his cock, her head thrown back in a delicious moan, her hands on her breasts, squeezing her nipples as she rode him with slow, torturous intent. Oh, yeah, he knew she was out to drive him crazy, and she was doing a damn fine job of it.

Thank God he'd come in the shower, because just looking at her naked body, her blond hair whipping around her shoulders, the more than obvious pleasure she was feeling, was enough to send him to the moon and back.

He gasped in a lungful of air as she settled fully on him. When she straightened and met his gaze, the fire in her eyes was as exciting as the way she gripped his length.

"I told you you would like me on top."

He nodded.

"So next time, what are you going to say?"

He opened his mouth, but no words came out.

Taylor laughed. Rose up just an inch. "I didn't quite get that."

"Please," he said, his voice sounding more like Darth Vadar than was comfortable. "Anything you want. Anything."

Her grin turned evil, and so did her laugh. But he didn't care because she was on the move again, lifting her body up until she almost lost him, then hesitating an agonizing minute, only to give him back the will to live as she lowered herself once more.

The only problem with this perfect moment was that he couldn't kiss her. But he wasn't complaining. In fact, he was more grateful than he'd ever been in his life.

Her hands went to his chest. He watched, amazed, as her eyes fluttered closed and her rhythm quickened.

"Come for me," he whispered, praying he'd last until she got off. "Come on, baby. Do it."

If she heard him, she gave no sign. But it didn't matter. Because she was speeding toward a climax and there was no turning back. As for him? He just hung on for dear life.

HALF AN HOUR LATER, Taylor tried to catch her breath while she stared at the sprinkler in the ceiling. The sex hadn't been a fluke. He'd…

What had he done to her? It was as if her orgasms had a password that only Ben knew. Frankly, and she'd never admitted this to anyone but her Eve's Apple group, she normally preferred getting off by herself. Her trusty vibrator had been there through thick and thin. It never tried too hard or crapped out before she was done. It never hogged the covers, or smirked when she wanted cold pizza afterwards. She liked the control, and, unlike most women she knew, she preferred going right to sleep after.

And here was Ben making her feel just plain sorry for her pitiful vibrator. The good old boy had done his best, but it was a distant second to making love to the man gasping to her right.

Three times. She'd come three times, and not just little whoopee orgasms, either. Big old honkin' O's that had hit her so hard she'd nearly blacked out. She wasn't exactly sure how he'd pulled off the feat, but my God, she was thrilled he had.

However, and it was a big however, the really impressive thing about the past two hours was that Ben had made her feel utterly, completely safe. She'd never been so unselfconscious with another human. Her sounds, her positions, her face. She'd given him her everything, warts and all. And loved every second of it.

The lovemaking wasn't *it*. The lovemaking was a result of *it*. So?

"Good God, woman, what have you done to me?"

She grinned. He sounded worse than she did. "I was just minding my own business."

"Like hell." He rolled over, attempting to adjust the hopeless covers, then tossing them to the floor. "You're so…"

"No. We're so…"

He nodded then wiped some stray hairs off his forehead. "And I need water. I think I lost five pounds."

"Honey, if it was that easy, I'd never leave the bedroom."

He pulled her close to him, close enough to nip her shoulder. "It's a deal."

She shifted so she could look him in the eyes. "Ben, this is serious."

"What do you mean? The condom didn't break, did it?"

"No."

"So why is it so serious?"

"Because I don't understand it. Us. This."

He stretched, kissed her gently on the lips. "Stop trying. Just let it be."

"I'm trying. I mean— You know what I mean."

"Listen, I have an idea about tomorrow. About

Steve and Lisa. Let's focus on them, okay? Give their situation our full attention. I bet while we're doing that, things will straighten out completely for both of us. Deal?''

She smiled. ''I think it's brilliant.''

''I think you're wonderful.''

''Hey, what's with the hand?''

''Nobody said we can't do this while we talk.''

She giggled, and tried to listen. She didn't do a very good job.

16

THE RIDE UP the elevator had taken them over fifteen minutes. Not because the Stratosphere was a thousand feet in the sky, but because there were so many people trying to get to the top.

Taylor held on to Ben's hand as they were guided to the line for Project XSky, the newest and scariest of the rides atop the downtown hotel. Along with the roller coaster and the Big Drop, Project XSky was crowded as hell, as more people than she'd thought possible wanted to have the stuffing scared out of them.

Steve had always been a huge fan of roller coasters and scary rides, having dragged her to amusement parks from the time they were kids, forcing her, upon the pain of being branded a ''girl'' to ride with him, despite the terror involved. Once he and Ben had hooked up, she'd been left alone to some degree, but still, whenever he had the opportunity, Steve would make her climb into one contraption or another. She'd never admit to him that she rather enjoyed the thrill. He got too big a kick out of her whining.

Today, though, Steve was just plain excited. Lisa was far less so. She'd been dubious when Ben had roused them early this morning. Of course, their destination had been a secret at that point.

When the cab took them to the Stratosphere, she'd put up a bit of a fight, but Steve had promised her she didn't have to actually go on any rides if she didn't want to. As far as Taylor could see, she was being a trouper, though. Which was interesting, considering Ben's plan.

Of course Ben knew all about Steve's penchant for dangerous thrills, and Taylor had agreed that it was a part of him that wouldn't please Lisa. So they would take him to an environment where the kid in him could come out and play, and when Lisa objected, he'd have a clear and vivid picture of what he was about to sign on for.

Taylor wished it didn't have to be this way, but dammit, Steve was her brother, and nothing was more important than his happiness. Yeah, he loved Lisa, but what was wrong with waiting awhile? Finding out what the pill business was all about? Giving them a chance to think this through?

"Oh, my God."

They had reached the long line for the XSky, and Lisa had clearly realized what the ride was all about. The thing, and Taylor couldn't figure out a better word to describe it, was like a big ramp off the side of the building. Eight people were strapped in, eight hundred sixty-six feet above the earth, for a ride that would take them twenty-seven feet over the edge. At the end, there was nothing between the rider and the very, very long drop. Except, of course, the seat belts and the contraption itself.

"It goes thirty miles an hour," Ben said. "They use a magnetic braking system, and redundant ratcheting. The whole thing's over in a few minutes, but man, what a rush."

Lisa's face paled a bit more. "No. It's insanity. What if something goes wrong?"

"Nothing'll go wrong," Steve said, his hand squeezing her waist. "They test this thing until the cows come home."

"It's not the cows I'm worried about. I hate this."

"It's fun." Steve turned her around so she faced him instead of the ride. "It's all about the adrenaline. Being scared in a safe environment. You'll never feel more alive, I swear."

"I'm very happy with my current feelings, thank you. And besides, I have so much to do. I mean, we're getting married tomorrow, remember?"

"What else is there to do? Your mom arranged all the flowers yesterday. We have the judge all set up. The clothes are bought." He kissed her on the lips, held her shoulders with his broad hands. "Just hang a little while longer, okay? If you decide not to ride, that's cool. But I don't want you to leave."

"I wasn't planning on going by myself," she said, her tone surprised.

He hadn't expected that. "Oh. Well." Steve cleared his throat, looked at Ben, then back at his bride-to-be. "All right. Sure. Let's go."

Lisa smiled, but as she watched Steve's dejection her grin faded. "No, no. I was just kidding. We can stay."

He lit up like a little kid. "You sure?"

She nodded, but Taylor could see this wasn't turning out to be a good morning for Lisa.

"So you don't care for thrill rides, Lisa?" she asked.

"God, no."

"Oh, man," Ben said. "Steve hasn't told you about his dream, huh?"

"What dream?"

They moved another inch along the ride. Screams wafted through the air, along with the sound of metal on metal as the rides started and stopped. The atmosphere, aside from being Vegas hot, was filled with the spice that always accompanied danger, and Taylor couldn't help but notice that the couples around her were all hanging on to each other.

She'd clung to Ben, wanting him close. The same should have been true for Lisa and Steve, but it wasn't. Steve touched Lisa, but her body language was all wrong. Defensive, distant. She didn't want to be here.

Taylor wanted Steve to see it, but she wondered if he could. Love was sometimes so blind. Even if she pointed out the differences between them, Steve would come up with rationales, reasons. Which wasn't a bad thing in itself, but what did it say for the long-term?

In her heart of hearts she knew this marriage was a mistake. But what if it was an important mistake? What if it was all part of Steve's journey toward the man he was supposed to become. They should just butt out.

Except...

She had to find out why Steve had taken those pills. And what they were for. That wasn't negotiable. "Tell you what, Lisa. Why don't you and I get out of line? I don't want to go on the horrible thing, either. Let the boys have their fun. I want to hear more about your decorating business anyway."

Lisa looked at her with genuine fondness. "That would be wonderful." She turned to Steve. "Okay?"

He folded her in him arms, and hugged her close. Taylor's resolve dropped another notch. God, who was she to try to fix anyone else's life? She could barely manage her own.

Steve gave a jaunty wave as he turned back to the line and Ben. Taylor scoped out a place where she and Lisa could sit and wait it out. There was a small bench near the elevator, which was almost empty. A woman was nursing her baby there, but Taylor didn't think that would be a problem.

Lisa sighed as she sat, checked that she could see the boys in line, then turned to Taylor. "So, you want to know about my decorating business, right?"

Taylor nodded. "I watch HGTV all the time, but I have no talent whatsoever. You should see my place. White walls, bland carpet, nothing truly original or fun. I have a few pieces I really like, that I found at flea markets. This great Vietnamese dragon carved from teak, and then there's this glass sculpture that makes me so happy, it's—"

"Taylor?"

"Yeah?"

"What did you really want to talk about?"

"Excuse me?"

Lisa scooted a bit closer. "I know you guys aren't thrilled about me and Steve. That you think this marriage is a mistake."

"No, no, not at all." She could feel her cheeks heat and wished like hell she was a better liar.

"I don't blame you. I came out of nowhere. I'm not part of the whole San Diego scene. We've only known each other for a few months. Should I go on?"

Taylor leaned her elbows on her knees. "Okay, so we're...concerned. We love Steven, okay? All we want is what's best for him."

"And I appreciate that. The thing is, I love him, too."

"Do you?"

"Taylor, this can't ever work if you're not going to believe me."

She sat up, rubbed the back of her neck. Damn, it was hot. "You're right. Again. In fact, I do believe you love him. What you know of him. And I believe he loves you. What I can't seem to reconcile is this new life he's leaping into. It's—"

"The opposite of everything he's ever said he's wanted?"

Taylor nodded.

"I know. We've talked and talked about it. I don't want him to be unhappy. In fact, I want him to be blissfully happy. And he says, over and over, that our life together is going to make him happy."

"He's always loved the boats, Lisa. He's lived for those boats. What happened?"

"Aside from me?"

Again, Taylor's cheeks heated. This wasn't going

as well as she could have hoped. On the other hand, there wasn't a lot of bullshit happening here, and that was a really good thing.

"I admit, love is a pretty powerful thing. But to give up everything he's ever loved?"

"If Ben asked you to give up your life to go with him, would you?"

Taylor burst out laughing. "Ben? Me? Are you kidding? We're not—"

"Now who's not telling the truth?"

"I admit, we're having ourselves a time, but it's not the same thing at all. Ben and I aren't in love."

Lisa nodded slowly. "Right."

"What is this?"

"Nothing."

"Hey."

Lisa smiled enigmatically. "No, no. My fault. You two are just having a good vacation. Catching up on old times. It doesn't mean a thing."

"It doesn't."

Lisa laughed. "There are no guarantees Steve and I are going to make it. Maybe we'll crash and burn, I don't know. But at least we're going to give it our all." She turned and took Taylor's hands in hers. "We talk. We do. Even though it's not easy for Steve to come right out and speak his heart, he's trying so hard. He wants a family, Taylor, and so do I. We want a secure, good life, something that has roots. He doesn't want to give up the boats. But he wants more. He wants everything he had as a boy, only this time, he wants to be the husband and father."

"I think that's wonderful. I do. Isn't there a way

to have all that, and still not put Steve in a suit and tie?"

"You don't think I suggested it?"

That caught Taylor completely by surprise. "You didn't?"

"Of course. I wasn't kidding when I said I want his happiness."

"But—"

"What?"

"Why here? Why so fast? I figured you were hurrying into this so Steve wouldn't have time to reconsider."

"Maybe we are. Maybe neither of us want too much time. Diving into the deep end, you know."

"Yeah. Kind of."

"It's not a bad way to go. As long as you know drowning's not an option."

Taylor sat staring at the line inching toward XSky. Ben and Steve weren't in her line of sight any longer. In fact, they might already be on the giant fulcrum thingy. She shivered, half glad, half sorry she'd begged out.

"Go with us on this, Taylor. Please. You mean so much to him. He won't say anything. He can't. But he's desperate for your approval. He needs your support."

"I do support him. We all do."

"You know what I think?" Lisa said. "I think Steve and I are going to be great. We're going to grow old together, and play with our great-great-grandkids. And Steve's gonna teach all of them to fish."

"I think, with you, he's got a fighting chance."

"But?"

"Will you please tell me what the deal is with the pills? What's wrong with Steve, and why is he being so secretive about it?"

Lisa didn't answer. Another batch of thrill seekers got off the ride, and Taylor was pretty sure she heard Steve's laugh. When she turned to tell her future sister-in-law that the boys were coming, she realized she'd managed to put her great big foot right in the middle of it.

Lisa's face was pale as ivory. Her mouth had opened slightly, and her breathing was too rapid. She clearly didn't know a thing about the pills, or why Steve was taking them. Not one thing.

BEN COULDN'T FIND his breath, let alone get it under control. And his guts were still somewhere over the edge of the Stratosphere. It felt like the top of his head had exploded, and the rest of his body had followed shortly thereafter.

"Holy shit," Steve said, leaning against the building, his right hand over his heart. "You think the girls would kill us if we did it again?"

"No, but I might kill you if you don't tell me what the hell is going on."

Steve's expression changed immediately. Gone was the breathless rush from the ride, replaced by the kind of anger Ben had rarely seen in his friend. "What the hell are you talking about?"

"If you don't know, why are you so pissed off?"

"God damn Taylor. I told her it was nothing." He tried to push off the wall, but Ben pushed him back.

"Stop it. Tell me the truth."

"Get out of my face, Ben."

"No. I'm your friend, damn you. What are the pills? What happened to you?"

"Nothing."

"Steve, don't make me beat the crap out of you."

He continued to push Steve against the wall, using his forearm in a modified choke hold. He wouldn't hurt him, but he wasn't going anywhere. "You've got family here, big guy, who care whether you live or die. So tell me what's going on."

"Nothing's going on. I'm fine."

"Bull."

Steve stopped struggling. The air seemed to deflate from his body. "Don't do this, man."

"Why not? Why shouldn't I get all over your ass? You're scaring your sister. And I happen to care about your sister."

"It's not what you think."

"How the hell do you know what I think?"

"All right. Let up. You're choking me."

Ben let go. Hating this. Wishing Steve would just tell him the truth so he wouldn't have this knot in his gut.

"Listen, to me. I'm okay. But I can't tell you."

"What?"

The whole line of people behind them turned to stare. Ben smiled at them, then pulled Steve behind a post. "What?"

"I have to talk to Lisa first."

"She doesn't know?"

He shook his head. "No one knows."

"God dammit, Steve. Just tell me you're not going to keel over at the ceremony, okay? That I don't have to put 9-1-1 on speed dial."

"It's not like that. Trust me."

"You're not making it easy."

"I know. But you gotta just chill. Don't make this more than it is. I'll talk to Lisa, I swear."

"When?"

"Soon."

Ben shook his head. "Not even close."

"All right. Tonight."

"Fine. Now let's go find them. Tell them what a great ride it was."

"Great, yeah."

Ben punched his friend in the arm. "Hey, you love her, don't you?"

"Lisa? Yeah."

"I mean, really love her."

Steve stopped. "What did you think? I'm not marrying her because of her comic book collection."

"She has a comic book collection?"

Steve slugged him back.

"Ow. Okay, okay. So I'm being a jerk. But jeez, Steve, Kansas?"

"Kansas isn't so bad."

"Not if you're corn."

Steve stopped. "I'm not giving up the fleet, man. I'm just changing directions. I'm doing what I should do. What I want to do. And I want to do it with Lisa."

Ben almost argued, but he didn't. He looked at

Steve's face and he saw something he'd never seen before. Whether it was maturity, determination or just a commitment to his course, the man wasn't kidding. "Hey."

"What?"

Ben held out his hand. "Best friend. Best man. Beside you all the way."

Steve took it. "I know you're concerned, but don't be. Just take care of yourself, okay?"

"What's that supposed to mean?"

Steve's hand gripped his tighter. "I see what's happening between you and Taylor."

"And what's that?"

Steve laughed. "Are you kidding?"

Ben pulled his hand back. "This isn't funny, man."

"Oh, I think it's really funny. Talk about pots calling kettles."

"You're out of your mind. Those pills are for psychosis right? Hallucinations?"

"Yeah, that's it. I'm the one that's nuts. Boy, are you in for a surprise."

"Look, there they are." Ben pointed to the girls, sitting on the bench. They look hot. And I mean that both ways."

"Fine. Have it your own way, but don't say I didn't warn you."

"Steve, my man, you're out of your friggin' mind."

"Tell you what," Steve said, pulling him to a stop. "Give me that notebook you hide in your pocket."

Ben didn't like it, but he took out the small pad he

used for notes and emergencies. Steve had his own pen. He wrote for a few seconds, hiding his hand so Ben couldn't see what was there. Then he tore out the page, folded it, and handed it to Ben along with the pen. "Initial it."

"What's it say?"

"None of your damn business. Just initial it. In your very best handwriting."

Ben did. But only because he couldn't figure out a way to get out of it.

Steve took it back, and with great fanfare, put it in his wallet. "We'll take a look at this baby just before we go home. And then, my man, if you can't call me a liar, then you owe me a beer."

"I'm not an idiot. And I can already call you a liar. It's not gonna happen."

"Don't say any more. Just wait."

"Steve, I like your sister a lot. But I'm not in love with her. I'm not going to be in love with her. This is a week. It's going to end. No big deal."

Steve nodded, then his grin faded sharply. Ben spun around, but he already knew what was behind him.

Taylor. Lisa. And they both looked as if their whole worlds had come crashing down around them.

17

LISA WAS THE FIRST to speak. "Steve?" Her voice sounded small, scared. "Honey, is there something wrong with you?"

Steve gave Taylor a scorching glare, then took his sweetheart to stand in the line for the elevator down. His arm went around her shoulders and he whispered earnestly while Lisa leaned against him.

Taylor, feeling crappy in all kinds of ways, turned to Ben. "So, did you have a fun ride?"

"Yeah. It was great. Scary as hell."

"Did you throw up?"

"No."

"Bummer," she said, then she headed toward the elevator herself, careful not to stand too close to her brother. Ben hadn't said a thing she didn't know, but his conviction had taken her about ten steps back.

She was no big deal.

Golly, she could have gone the rest of her life without hearing that. Because to her, Ben was a big deal. One of the biggest. Growing bigger by the second.

She'd thought the guys were talking about the ride. Kidding around. Certainly not discussing her. When she'd overheard his vehement denial, all her defenses had risen. The nights they'd shared, her own confession to him, she'd thought they meant something. Certainly more than he did.

"Taylor?"

"Yeah?" she said, not looking back to see him right behind her. She sure as hell felt him though. Felt his heat, his pull on her. Why? Why did she give him so much power when he obviously didn't want anything more than the boink-a-thon she'd promised him?

"Hey, I didn't mean anything by that stuff, you know. It was Steve. He was trying to deflect the conversation away from him and Lisa."

Ben slipped in front of her, not giving her a chance to escape or even turn. His hands held her arms steady, directly facing him. But she wouldn't meet his gaze.

"Hey, come on. You know you mean a lot to me."

She raised her eyes enough to see he was trying to tell the truth. "I know. And don't worry, my panties aren't in a twist or anything. I'm just tired."

He nodded, but his concerned expression told her he wasn't buying it. "Let me take you to lunch, and then—"

"No, that's okay. I'm just going to go back to my room to get some rest. We have that dinner tonight, remember?"

"Oh, yeah. Tomorrow is the big day."

She nodded for him to step along with the line. They should be next to get in the elevator. "So what happened with you and Steve?"

By the time he'd filled her in, they were off the elevator, waiting in another line for a cab. When she'd given her own blow-by-blow of her conversation with Lisa, they were back at the Hard Rock.

"Let me take you to the Pink Taco," Ben said.

"Thanks, but no."

They walked in silence into the hotel, past the registration desk. As always, the casino was hopping, the music was rocking, and everyone seemed to be having the time of their lives. All she wanted was to crawl into a cave. Her bed would do, the bathtub would be better, and figure out what the hell she was doing to herself. This was nuts.

Sure, Ben had been a presence all her life, but she'd never realized how deeply he'd affected her. What was all the more disturbing was what she'd made him out to be. He'd become a symbol, a reason, an excuse, all without his permission.

It was time to get real about Ben. About her life. Today, not tomorrow. She leaned over and kissed Ben briefly on the mouth. "I'm going," she said. "I want some time alone. You go have fun, and I'll see you tonight, okay?"

He didn't look happy about it, but he nodded.

She headed straight to the elevator. Alone.

Ben watched her disappear, kicking himself for his own stupidity. Not simply because he'd said that crock of nonsense to Steve, but because he hadn't been able to get out of it with any grace or dignity. He didn't care what kind of a fool he made of himself, but the last thing on earth he wanted to do was hurt Taylor.

How true that was had become increasingly apparent as they'd taken the journey back to the Hard

Rock. He gave a considerable damn what Taylor thought of him, and cared even more that he make her happy.

Which scared the hell out of him.

He'd wanted his ex to be happy, sure. But it hadn't felt like this. Nothing had ever felt like this. Symptoms? An overwhelming desire to touch, to caress, to make love. The inability to stop thinking about her. The completely odd sensation of caring more about her happiness than his own.

He didn't want to go to his room. Too many opportunities to think up there. But he also didn't feel like gambling. Sightseeing?

He tried to think what was real close. Everything. Including the New York, New York. Which had an excellent arcade, or so he'd read.

Yes. He'd buy himself some tokens and go kill dinosaurs or zombies, or throw baskets or darts. He had several hours until dinner, and an arcade was just the ticket.

SHE MIXED HER BATH with jasmine oil and when it was all hot and steamy and smelling gorgeous she slowly sank into the water, two candles lit nearby sitting next to a bottle of minibar wine and a chocolate bar.

Thoughts of Ben, what he meant to her, what was real and imagined, what was pretense and what was in her heart, spun in her head. So many years, so much thought, but how much of it was about the real Ben versus the Ben she'd made up?

Back then, when she'd been eighteen, she'd

thought him to be the perfect man. Aside from the whole looks thing, there was more to love about him than anyone she'd ever met. His kindness to her, and to most people. She remembered this one kid that was in her brother's class, who was slightly autistic. Shunned by almost everyone, Ben had befriended the boy—Alec, his name was—and they'd played chess together. Alec had worshipped Ben, and Ben had accepted him completely. Then others had behaved better toward Alec because Ben was also the coolest of the high school jocks.

And not just a jock. He'd been smart, a leader even though he never sought out the role. People naturally had followed him, that's all, because even at that age he was so thoroughly his own man.

Later, in his senior year, he'd driven himself to excel even in areas he'd found difficult. She remembered him struggling through chemistry, hiring a tutor. She'd never forget that because the tutor had been this buxom redhead who was more interested in their personal chemistry than what was in the texts, and Taylor had been swamped by jealousy.

Ben had always asked about her. Sent her these weird postcards from wherever he'd happened to be. Most of them said, ''Wish you were here,'' and she'd believed the cards, if not him. She still had them all, in a small shoebox in her armoire.

He'd been so good for Steven. Encouraging, tough when necessary. And how he made her brother laugh.

When she'd found out Ben had gotten married, she'd been miserable for way too long. Months and months. As if he'd jilted her, even though that wasn't the case at all. She'd felt as if something had been ripped from her heart, and frankly, the feeling had never totally gone away.

Ben belonged to her. That was the bottom line. She'd believed that since the age of ten, and no distance between them or time lapsed could change it.

She let her head loll back and closed her eyes. A life without Ben was incomprehensible. A life with Ben, real Ben, close, together, gliding through days of ups and downs, through the mundane and the spectacular, was quite simply the most perfect idea ever.

Her eyes came open and her breathing stopped. *Oh, God.* Ben hadn't been her excuse. Well, he had, but not for the reasons she'd thought. He'd been her excuse because she was in love with him. Had been in love with him forever. Would be in love with him until the end of her days.

No wonder no other man had had a chance.

No wonder Ben was never far from her thoughts.

No wonder this week was doomed to fail from the start.

Okay. So she knew. She couldn't deny it, couldn't alter it, couldn't forget it.

Now what?

THE FIRST THREE ZOMBIES died from a single gunshot wound to the center of the forehead. The fourth got it right in the heart. And Ben was using his left hand.

He switched to his right, and zombies dropped like flies. The graphics on the game were quite good. Fast-moving, nice mobility, cool dimensionality. Better than the cop game he'd finished a few minutes ago.

Unfortunately, the zombie game was one of the most popular, and he was surrounded by a gang of middle-school kids, impressed by his shooting skills, but all wanting their turn.

He finished the game, toting up an impressive score, then headed toward the fairway games. Tossing a basketball felt about his speed. And he could be relatively alone, as most all the crowd wanted higher-tech thrills.

Taylor.

He put the money in the slot, and the basketballs rolled down. His first throw tanked, but the second was all air.

Taylor.

What the hell? He continued to throw, but paid little attention to the results. What was it about her? And what was it that Steve had seen? That he liked his sister? Sure, yeah, he did. A lot. More than he had anyone in a long, long time. Being with her was exciting, excellent. He didn't want the week to end. So what?

So what.

He put more money in the machine. Started back throwing. Moving his legs a bit, getting fancy. Missing. He went back to a straight free throw.

Back home, he had a full plate. Joe Panzer, the Stigler case, estate hunting for an old woman who lived like she didn't have a dime, but in fact was worth in excess of four million bucks. A psychology course at NYU. Lots of stuff. Fun, fun, fun.

Alone, alone, alone.

He threw the ball so damn hard it bounced out of

its protected netting, hitting a teenager wearing huge jeans and a Kid Rock T-shirt.

"Sorry, man."

"Cool it, dude," the boy said, shaking it off.

"Yeah. Okay." He took the ball, put it back on the rack. Headed toward the escalator.

At the casino level, Ben walked aimlessly, admiring the Art Deco decor, the brilliant colors. He had no desire to play any of the machines and no wish to visit the bar. But there was a hell of a nice big leather chair in the lobby with no one around.

He sank into the overstuffed cushion, and it made him think of home. He'd gotten his neighbor, Mrs. Pershing, to feed his fish and take in his mail. Collect his newspapers.

But when he got back, he knew just what he'd find. The same old same old. Life, or at least his own version of life. Making a big deal out of his morning coffee. Reading the *Times* like it mattered. Following up on his leads, wrapping up cases, getting new cases, giving up on the hopeless cases.

Going to bed alone. Or worse, going to a bar, meeting someone he didn't want to know just to have a little human contact.

Was this what he'd signed up for? What he'd dreamed of as a kid? He'd wanted to make a difference back then, and he hadn't been kidding. So what had happened?

He'd learned, early on, to keep his emotions to himself. To guard against caring. People lie. People do bad things. It didn't pay to trust.

And then, with Alyson, there had been moments.

Infrequent at best. They'd had the occasional meal. They'd talked about her day, his day, but there had always been a distance between them. Sex had been okay for him, an act for her.

Nothing remotely like being with Taylor.

He closed his eyes, his head running a movie he'd never seen before. Him, having his morning coffee, only this time, Taylor had his *Far Side* cup, while he had his *Get Fuzzy* mug. Her, laughing. Asking him where he'd be, when he'd be home. Could he stop at the market and pick up some milk. Him, going through his cases, only this time, he'd stop at one and make a quick phone call. "Hey, Taylor, how's it going, honey? You got that tort done? Fantastic. See you tonight."

Thinking of her again at four, at the station. In the cells that smelled of all the bad things you can think of, but he had a scent in his head that he could pull on, run with. Her scent.

Stopping at the little grocery on the corner, getting the milk and picking up some fresh flowers because Taylor was crazy about mums. Unlocking his door, a smile on his face instead of the steady numbness. Not even thinking about the tube, or if he'd run out of clean socks.

Taylor, greeting him with a smile and a hug, and her warmth and her love and her passion and her humor. Taylor, giving a damn about his day. Telling him stuff that he wouldn't have cared about except that it had happened to her, and she was his, and everything mattered. Every detail. All the mundane crap, the sirens, the crime rate, the screaming downstairs neighbors, the dentist, all of it meaning something because it was her. Taking care of himself not because he needed to outrun the bad guys but because he wanted to be healthy for as long as possible because life wasn't something to wait out, but something precious.

Taylor.

She could change everything. She could mean everything. But what about her end of the bargain? What would she get?

Him.

Not fair. Not in the least fair.

DINNER WAS AT BARABAS. Amazingly, it wasn't the fanciest or the noisiest restaurant on the strip. It was a cozy Italian place with a decent wine list and the scent of parmesan cheese and tomatoes in the air. The table was large enough to accommodate the whole gang, Lisa, Steve, Pauline, Mimi and then, of course, her and Ben.

He looked so gorgeous. Black jeans, crisp white shirt, bolo tie, black jacket. Hair pushed back, cheekbones for days, his eyes full of signs and wonders.

"You look stunning," he whispered as he pulled the big chair out for her. She adored the simple courtesy of him behind her chair, loved that he didn't use any kind of cologne.

"Thank you," she said as his hands ran up the length of her arms before he circled the table and sat across from her.

Steve and Lisa were on her left, the mothers on her right. The lovebirds looked as if all was well. Steve must have told all to his bride, and she clearly was cool with the prognosis. At least there weren't secrets going into the marriage. And from her seat far off in the bleachers, it seemed like the two of them had a real good shot at making it work. Who was she to question anything about love? In that regard, she was a misguided fool at best.

She talked to her mom, who had been in a perfect frenzy of bingo until all hours for the past few days. She'd won a grand, of which she had about two hundred left.

"Mom, you've spent eight hundred dollars on bingo?"

"And I intend to spend two hundred more before I go home. I'm on vacation. My son is getting married. I can have wine spritzers for breakfast if I want, and there's nothing anyone can do about it."

"You're right. Good for you."

"Thank you. Now, tell me what's going on between you and Ben."

"What?"

"I'm not on the moon. Steve tells me you two are getting hot and heavy."

"Mom!"

She grinned, looking a lot younger than she had at the beginning of the trip. "Spill, child."

"Fine. We're not. Hot. Or Heavy. We're just having a wonderful vacation that's going to be over very shortly. That's all."

Her mother grunted. Something else new. "I don't buy it."

"Buy it."

The waitress came by, and Taylor ordered the spaghetti marinara with a salad on the side. Her mom got lasagna and Ben ordered ravioli and sausage. She didn't hear the rest of the orders and barely heard her mother until she got poked in the side. "What?"

"Why are you so sad? Did he say something? Do something?"

"I'm not sad."

"You're my daughter. I know when you're unhappy. That makeup isn't hiding a thing. You're miserable. It's not about Steve, is it?"

"No."

"Then?"

She sighed. Leaned closer to her mother's ear. "Ben said I'm no big deal."

"Oh."

"So can we just enjoy our meal, please?"

"Honey, I haven't butted into your life for a long time."

"Yeah, weeks, at least."

"Shh. Listen. Don't leave this place without telling him how you feel."

"Why? Because my humiliation isn't on a grand enough scale?"

"No. Because you'll hate yourself if you don't."

"Mom, I love you, but you don't know what you're talking about. Hey, look over there," she said, pointing at nothing across the way.

"Subtle, darling." Her mother patted her hand, showing off some very vivid red nail polish. "I may not know very much about the world, but I know you. And for once in your life, listen to your mother.

Okay? Now, what do you say, let's have a toast to the happy couple.''

Taylor picked up her wine, and so did the rest of the guests. Steve stood up. Smiled. ''Thanks you guys. For everything.'' He lifted his glass, looked at Lisa, then back at his family. ''The wedding's off.''

18

GUILT, LIKE A HOT KNIFE, sliced through Taylor as the words sank in. She'd meddled, they'd all meddled, and look what happened. Two people who clearly loved each other were calling off their future. She wanted to stand up, take it all back, beg them to reconsider. Instead, she took hold of her mother's hand while Steve continued.

"Let me rephrase that," he said, smiling again at Lisa, then looking back. "This wedding's off. We're still going to get married."

Taylor exhaled, the relief enough to make her dizzy.

"Why?" Ben asked. "Everything's all set to go."

"Because we want to do this right," Steve said. He sat down, leaned in to the table. The spark that Taylor had seen only in bits and snatches was back in his eyes, and he looked like the Steve of old. So maybe this was the right thing. Maybe they hadn't screwed things up too badly.

"We're going to get married in Kansas, so Lisa's dad can be there. So her friends can be there." He covered her hand with his. "So she can say goodbye."

"What?" Mimi, who seemed awfully pasty, blinked

several times. She looked as if she'd been mugged. "But the chapel. The judge. The flowers. It's all ready. Tomorrow night, seven o'clock. There's an organist. And a photographer."

"And we'll pay for all that, Mom," he said. "But tell the truth, wouldn't you rather us get married at your church, with all your friends there? We can have the reception at the club, just like you wanted us to do."

"I suppose," she said unconvincingly. She drank the wine in her glass and reached for the bottle.

Ben got it first, and filled her glass. "What was that about saying goodbye?"

"A lot has happened since yesterday," Lisa said. "Steve has something else to share."

Steve kept his gaze on Lisa. "I'm sorry I didn't say something before, but... Anyway, about four months ago I had a heart attack."

Taylor gasped, checked on her mother, whose pallor now matched Mimi's.

"Don't everybody freak. It turns out it was a good thing. I had something wrong with the lining of my heart, but they caught it in time and repaired it. I'm lucky."

"You went through it alone?" Ben asked. "You didn't tell anyone?"

"Larry was there. He took me to the hospital. Just in time, it turns out. But here's the deal. I'm better than ever, now. Honest. They fixed it, and the doc said there's no reason I should have any trouble again. Hey, I figure it could have happened at sea, and then I'd have been a goner. I got a second chance."

"And that's why you wanted to do all this," Taylor said. "Hurry up and get married. Start a family."

"Yeah. Let me tell you, it scared the hell out of me. But once Lisa and I talked about it, and she finished yelling at me, we took another look at the big picture."

Lisa squeezed his hand. "I've known from the first moment I met him that he loved his boats more than anything."

"Almost anything," Steve added.

"Right." Lisa focused on her mother, who was having the most difficult time with all this. "The point is, even though I think he'd do wonderfully at whatever he set his mind to, being a sales rep for Dad's company wouldn't have made him truly happy. And that's all I want for him. Besides, I like the weather in San Diego."

"You're moving?" Mimi asked.

"Yes. I'm sorry, Mom, I know it kind of leaves you in the lurch, but I know you'll do fine. You have so many friends, and there's no reason you can't go on with the business. I'm going to start up something in California. And in the meantime, I'll help Steve however I can."

"We're gonna buy a house, though. That's the first order of business."

Taylor looked at Ben who seemed to be in a state of shock. A happy state, from the looks of it. "What I can't understand," she said, "was why all the secrecy?"

Steve shook his head. "I don't know. According to Lisa, stupidity pretty much covers it."

"Well," Taylor's mom said, "I'm thrilled. I think this is an excellent beginning. A wonderful start to a happy life. You both have my full support. Whatever I can do to help." She lifted her glass to the couple, then turned pointedly toward Mimi.

She wasn't so eager to give her blessings, but she did, after finishing her wine.

The food arrived, and for a while all everyone did was eat. But Ben kept sneaking glances at her, then turning away. He had to be happy with all this. Steve had told the truth, they weren't rushing into an ill-advised marriage, and he wasn't giving up his dreams. And yet, she could tell that something was bothering him. She wished they'd sat next to each other. She'd corner him after dinner, that's all.

Lisa rapped her spoon against her glass to get everyone's attention. "Ladies, don't forget, tomorrow morning we still have our appointments at the spa."

"But why?" Mimi looked so forlorn. All her plans had become so much dust.

"Just because we're not getting married, doesn't mean this can't still be a celebration. Tomorrow night, we're taking you and Pauline to dinner and a show. Celine Dion."

Mimi brightened right up. "How? The tickets are impossible."

"Steve came through. Turns out the concierge loves deep-sea fishing, and he's going to be joining us on a trip to Baja next month. Sorry it couldn't have been tickets for us all."

"Hey, that's fine," Ben said. "I'm sure we'll come up with something to occupy our time."

Steve waggled his eyebrows. "You know, it's not too late to change our minds. Keep the chapel and everything."

Ben looked like he'd been slapped. His eyes widened in panic. Taylor could have killed Steve. It had all been going so well. She coughed, trying to cover her embarrassment and excused herself. The walk to the rest room took a million years, all of which were filled with humiliation and a sadness that went straight to her bones.

She wished like hell Steven hadn't made the joke. Not just for the obvious reason, but because at that second she realized that more than anything in the world, all she had wanted was for Ben to say yes.

BEN GOT THROUGH the rest of dinner, although at the end he couldn't have said what he ate or how it tasted. The mixture of guilt and anger had dulled his senses, and all he wanted was to escape.

What the hell was he supposed to have done? Said sure, I'd love to marry your sister, even though we haven't seen each other in ten years, but gee, the sex is great, so I know it has to work out? What the hell was Steve thinking, making a crack like that. It would have been stupid enough to say it privately, but with Taylor sitting right there?

Ben hardly ever got mad at Steve, but tonight was the exception. Boy, was it an exception. The bastard had put him in a tight corner with no escape routes. Of course he knew Taylor would have laughed him out of the room if he'd even suggested that they jump into marriage like that. She was a sensible girl, and even though she was going through a lot of emotional stuff with him, she hadn't once said she was in love with him.

Even if she had, that wouldn't mean they should, well, get married, for God's sake. Marriage was big. Huge. Important. Forever.

Everyone else was already standing, waiting to leave. He got up, followed them out of the restaurant, making sure he wasn't next to Taylor.

At the curb, waiting for taxis, he gave himself a mental chuck to the head and went over to her. "Hey."

She smiled, but it seemed strained to him. "Sorry about that."

"About what?"

She looked at him as if he was a total jerk. Which was true.

"Oh, yeah. You don't need to apologize. However, I do plan on kicking your brother's ass from here to the hotel."

"He doesn't say much, but when he does, it's a doozy."

"Yeah. I mean, come on. Us? Get married? Tomorrow? What's he, crazy?"

She looked down the street. "Yeah, crazy."

"What are you up to now?" he asked.

"I think I'm just gonna go to bed. I'm pretty tired, and I have to get up early to do the whole spa thing."

"Ah, yeah. The spa thing. What does that include, exactly?"

She still kept an eye out for oncoming cabs. "Manicure, pedicure, facial, hair, makeup. The whole wedding package.''

''Well, then, I guess I better get cracking on something special for us to do tomorrow night.''

She turned to him finally. ''No. I mean, don't bother. You don't have to worry about me.''

''Worry about you? Are you kidding? I can't think of anything I'd rather do than escort you in all your glory. I just hope I can come up with something worthy.''

She smiled. ''Thanks, but really. Don't go to any trouble.''

He touched her arm, and she flinched. Not a big old jump backward, but he hadn't imagined it. ''What's wrong?''

''Nothing.''

He took her by the arms and pulled her away from the others. ''Taylor, come on. Talk to me.''

''It's nothing. I'm just tired.''

''I know you better than that. I think you're upset about what Steve said.''

''Well, of course. He's my brother, and he had a heart attack. Naturally, I'm worried.''

''That's not what I meant, and you know it.''

''Ben, drop it, okay? Please?''

He looked at her hard, wishing he were suave and clever and that he could say a few words that would set everything right. But he wasn't. All he knew was that he cared a hell of a lot about her, and he didn't want to make her sad. ''Tell you what,'' he said. ''Let's go back to the hotel, but instead of you going to your room alone, let's us have some fun. There's supposedly a really good dance club there. What say we shake it for a while? Get some ya-yas out?''

She laughed. It wasn't fake or anything, and he felt instantly better.

''I'm really not in the mood for any ya-ya shaking. But you're right. Let's do something fun.''

''There's a cool arcade at New York, New York.''

''Try again.''

''Miniature golf?''

She shook her head.

''How about a drive?''

''In what?''

''Let me worry about that. You go on up to your room, get into something comfy. I'll pick you up, and take you for a spin.''

She leaned forward and kissed him gently on the mouth. ''The cab is here.''

It took him a second to register what she'd said. ''Okay, then. Let's move.''

TAYLOR PUT ON the green dress. She thought about wearing something different, but she needed to feel good. The dress helped, but just a bit.

Her depression was irrational, she knew that. What on earth had she expected? Just because she loved Ben didn't mean he loved her. She knew he cared for her, but he had a whole life back in New York, and he'd said time and again that he didn't want a relationship.

Even if they could get past that, what would it mean? Trips back and forth between coasts? She had savings, but she was by no means wealthy. Who knew what Ben's finances were like. It would cost a fortune, and besides, long-distance relationships rarely worked out.

She finished in the bathroom, and got her computer from the bedroom. Settling herself on the curved couch, she booted up and went in to check her e-mail. There were several notes from the gang, and one was about her and Ben.

To: Taylor
From: Sandra
EvesApple.com
Subject: Discoveries

Dear Taylor,
I've been following your adventures with Ben, and I've decided to tell you what I've been thinking, and not sugarcoat it. Okay, so it's easier to be brave when it's someone else's life at stake, but here goes anyway.

I think you need to tell Ben you love him. What, you say? You never said anything about love?

Well, here's a news flash girlfriend: You're in love with Ben Bowman, and you have been for ten years.

Now, don't get all huffy. Maybe you can't see it, but damn girl, we can. The whole reason you haven't found the right man out there is because you already have the right man. Ben's been your guy, will be your guy. As far as I'm concerned, it's destiny, and you two just have to work out the details.

But, you say, he doesn't want a relationship! Yeah, yeah, heard that before. Here's another cosmic truth: Men don't know bupkis about what they want. They have to be shown. I'm sure Ben's a wonderful guy in all kinds of ways, but he's still clueless. It's up to you, babe, to show him the light.

Tell him that you love him. Don't wait for him to tell you he loves you back. That may take some time. Just believe it's true, and move on from there.

You've been living a half-life in San Fran. I know you have, because (and don't make me get out old e-mails to show you) you've said so time and again. There's nothing holding you there at all. The job? When's the last time you were passionate about that? Your pals? Just how easy has it been to take a pass at an evening out? Sure, you have your pool league, but guess what, they have pool leagues in New York. Your bike? They have roads in New York, too.

Tell the absolute truth now. If Ben asked you tonight to come live with him, what would you say? I already know the answer. You'd be on it like white on rice.

So don't wait for him to make the first move. You're a twenty-first-century woman. Take the bull by the horns, so to speak, and make your intentions known. I promise, Ben will be grateful.

The bottom line? Ben isn't your Man To Do. He's your Man To Keep.

So put your fears on the back burner, and get cooking. You have a life to live, and you'll never forgive yourself if you chicken out.

But, you ask, what if he says no? Then you're no worse off than you are now.

Why are you still reading? Go on. Go!

Your friend, Sandy.

Taylor didn't even realize she was crying until a big fat drop landed on the keyboard. She wiped her cheek and closed the e-mail.

Sure, it was easy for Sandy, for her mom to tell her to go for it. It was all simple when you're sitting in the bleachers. She was on the ten-yard line, here, and the chances of her getting creamed were damn good.

The truth was, she'd already been as brave as she could be. Braver than she ever thought she could. She'd told Ben about her confusion, about him being her reason, she'd even confessed about Cade. What did everyone want from her? She wasn't a superheroine. She wasn't even Mediocre Heroine. She was just Taylor, who'd been hiding from the truth for years and years, who'd been living in her safe little world, never facing the facts about her heart.

All she had to do was get through two more days. Then she could go back home and do everything in her power to get on with it. Forget about Ben, and all he'd been with her.

Okay, so it wasn't possible to forget about him, but she could put it all in perspective. Go out and meet new people with new eyes. She didn't have to continue to live in purgatory. She could change her life, all by her lonesome.

Oh, God. Lonesome.

The tears welled again, and that wasn't okay. She headed back to the bathroom, afraid of what she'd see in the mirror. She would not be a crying fool when Ben came to get her. In fact, she wasn't going to let him see any part of her emotional baggage. He didn't deserve that.

Ben had been nothing but a sweet pea the whole time they'd been here. All this was on her head. Her own damn fault.

Ben Bowman, aside from everything else, was a friend. A good friend. Someone who cared about her, who always would. She'd be a jerk to let that go because she couldn't have everything she wanted.

She worked some voodoo on her makeup, grateful that she wasn't a swollen mess. And just in time. The knock at the door came a few seconds after she'd powdered her nose. Pasting a big smile on her face, she opened the door to the man she would love forever.

Her heart shattered a wee bit more as she saw the bouquet of roses in his hand. He really was her dream guy. She simply wouldn't let it become a nightmare.

19

BEN WAITED WHILE TAYLOR filled the vase with water, and put it on the coffee table. He hadn't meant to make her cry. In fact, he'd wanted her to feel better.

"They're so beautiful," she said, wiping her eyes. "I love roses."

"They're not half as beautiful as you," he said, folding her into his arms. He kissed her, grateful when she sank against him.

For a long moment, all he did was appreciate the taste of her, the feel of her. He'd made such a mess of things, and he wanted to make it right. Tonight, he'd take her to play pool. He'd already made sure he could get a table at Pink-ees. They'd play, have some laughs, and by tomorrow, all would be well.

She pulled back, looked at him with glistening eyes. "I'm sorry."

"For what?"

"For being such a sap."

"What are you talking about?"

She sniffed. "Nothing. Never mind." She slipped away to get her purse. "I'm ready. Where are we going?"

"Well, remember you said you wanted to—"

"Wait." Taylor put her purse down again. "Don't say anything, okay? Just let me tell you what I have to."

"Sure."

She shook her head. "Don't say anything."

He almost spoke, but ended up nodding.

"Sit down."

He obeyed.

She didn't join him. Instead, she walked halfway across the room. Turned to face him. Opened her mouth. Shut it again. Then turned away.

He wasn't sure what to do. But he went with keeping quiet.

She turned back. Her spine was straight as a stick, her head upright, her hands twisting in front of her. She looked as if she was facing a firing squad. "Okay, so here it is. The truth. And you don't have to do anything with it. You don't even have to respond. It's my problem, not yours, so don't feel like you owe me anything."

He opened his mouth, but a hand raised sharply stopped him.

"If you interrupt, I won't be able to do this, so just sit there and listen. I've figured out some things these last few days. A lot of things. And trust me, it wasn't easy."

She walked four steps, turned around, came back the same distance. Only looking at him briefly, then studying the carpet or the wall. "I told you about why I wanted to sleep with you. And how that didn't work out so well. I mean, it worked out great, but not for me, you know?" She shook her head. "No, it was fantastic, better than wonderful… Oh, crap. I'm doing this all wrong.''

''It's okay.''

She glared at him, and he sank back on the couch.

After a deep breath, she started pacing again. ''Bottom line. That's always good, right? The bottom line. Here it is. I love you.''

He opened his mouth. Shut it again. Shocked more by the surge of happiness that shot through him than by the words themselves.

''For real. I'm talking love. The kind that changes everything. The kind that makes you want to spend the rest of your life with a person. Only, I didn't just fall in love with you. I've always been in love with you. Since I was eighteen. Or before that. I'm not sure of the date, but it's been a really, really long time, and nothing has changed it. Not living thousands of miles away, not being apart for years at a time, not dating other men, nothing. It's you. It's always been you, and there's not a damn thing I can do about it. But I know you don't want a relationship, and I can accept that. I'll go home and I won't even bother you. I'm not sure how, but I'll get over this thing. Maybe now that I know what's really happening, I'll have a decent chance of moving on.''

''Can I say something?''

''No!''

He held up both hands. ''Okay.''

''I just figured you had a right to know. And I couldn't leave here without telling you because, and here comes another bottom line. You're my friend, Ben, you've always been my friend. From the time I made you teach me to slow dance. From the time I seduced you. From the moment I met you.''

She looked at him, a mixture of fascination and horror on her face. "Oh God! I didn't even see it. Until right this second. I've been the one... The whole time. It was me."

"What was you?"

"I tagged after you. I was the one with the crush. I asked you to teach me to dance. Forced you, really. I was the one to show up on your doorstep, begging you to make love to me. It was always me, never you. You were sweet and kind and you never made me feel like I was pushy or obnoxious or anything. But you never made a move. Until I'd asked. Until I'd begged."

Her hands went up to her face. "I'm such a moron. I never... Oh, God."

He'd had enough. He got up, went to Taylor, and pulled her hands from her face. "You through?"

She nodded. Then shook her head. Then nodded again.

"Good, because now it's my turn."

She closed her eyes.

"Look at me, Taylor."

She opened her left eye.

"All the way."

She did. Kind of. She squinted, though. It was good enough.

"I'm not in the least sorry that you asked me to teach you to dance. It's one of my favorite memories. Of course, it doesn't come close to the memory of the weekend we spent together, which, I figured, came about because I'd been very, very good in a past life. I certainly didn't deserve it in this one.''

''Every single time you've entered my world, you've made it better. Infinitely better. This week has been a revelation. Do you know what I did yesterday?''

She shook her head, and as she did, her eyes widened, her mouth parted slightly, and her expression became rapt.

''You know how I make up lives? For other people, for myself? Remember James Bond? All that?''

She nodded.

''Well yesterday, that's exactly what I did. I made up a life. My life. And you were there. You lived with me in New York. You had a job. We had coffee together. You had the *Far Side* mug, by the way. And we kissed before I left for work. And I got to think about you while I was out on the streets, and I got to call you when it was lunchtime, and I got to stop and pick up milk on the way home. It was as if I'd never seen the city before. As if I'd never understood my work, my life. Because all through the day, you were there. You were waiting for me. You changed that utilitarian co-op into a home, and me into a whole person, a real person, with a reason and a purpose. And when I came home, you were there, and we talked about the day, and I couldn't wait to hear what had happened to you. How you'd finished a damn tort. And everything I'd done was interesting because you cared about it.

''The best damn part of all was that I got to spend the rest of the night with you. And the night after that. In this universe I made up, you were there, for the good times and the bad. It changed everything. You changed everything.

"And you know what? I was a total jackass, sitting on that couch, making this wonderful scenario up in my head. Because I was too stupid, too afraid to take it out of pretend. To come right back to find you, to ask you— No, to beg you, to come to New York with me. To live with me in my stupid co-op. Because what I have now is nothing. It's a pretense of a life. A meaningless blur of days and nights that are so empty I can't see the bottom of them.

"All the time, you were here. Right here in front of me. I should have known it from the second I was inside you. I thought maybe it was the sex, isn't that a riot? That you had some magic when it came to making love. I think I mentioned I'm not very bright. Because if I'd had a brain, I would have seen that you and me, we're supposed to be together. But I didn't see. Until two minutes ago, when you said—"

She held up her hand once more to stop him. Took a very deep breath and let it go as the seconds ticked by. His heart beat so fast he thought maybe he was having one of those attacks that were so popular these days, but in truth, he just wanted her answer.

She smiled. "Okay," she whispered.

"Okay?"

She nodded, as another batch of tears came sliding down her perfect cheeks.

"You mean, you'll come to New York?"

"Yes."

"You'll take the *Far Side* mug?"

She laughed. "Yes."

"Well, then," he said. And then he kissed her.

One Year Later...

"You want more coffee?"

Taylor shook her head. "I don't want to be late. I've got that Simmons brief to write and Dan is breathing down my neck."

Ben poured himself another cup in his *Get Fuzzy* mug. He sat back down at the dining room table, his gaze settling on the small bouquet of football mums in the blue glass vase. Taylor's touch. There was so much of it now in the apartment, it felt as if he was living in a different place. A much better place. Ever since she'd moved here, his life had transformed into something he barely could have imagined. That one day, sitting in Las Vegas, on that leather couch, had been a clue, but he'd been incapable of visualizing how good it could get.

Who knew Taylor would love the city this much? That she'd find such a great job, only one subway stop away? More than that, how could he have guessed that having her in his life would change him from the inside out. He hadn't known this happiness before, not ever. Looking forward to her every day, making love to her, hearing her voice on the phone. It was better than he deserved by a long shot.

She was happy, too. He saw it in her smile, the way she carried herself, the joy in her voice when he walked in the door. This was the kind of love he'd read about, but never believed was real.

She stood up, looking so fine in her tan slim skirt and her white blouse. Nothing fancy, but her beauty made it spectacular. God, how he loved her.

"Okay, so what time will you be home tonight?" she asked.

"Nine, if I'm lucky."

"Should I wait?"

"Naw. Eat. I'll be fine."

She came over to his side of the table and kissed him. Instead of a peck, the kiss lingered, and he felt himself stir, as always. The woman did things to him. Every damn time.

"I've got to run."

As she turned, he caught her hand. "Wait."

She looked at him, brows raised.

"Didn't you tell me you were getting some time off from that job of yours?"

"Yep. My first vacation. A whole week. Why? Did you have something you wanted to do?"

He nodded. "Yeah."

"Well?"

He pulled her around and lowered her onto his lap. "I was thinking we could go back to Vegas."

He saw the disappointment in her eyes. She'd mentioned Hawaii, and he'd seen the brochures she'd hidden in her bedside drawer. "Oh," she said. "You want to do Vegas again?"

"Well, I figure it would be pretty easy to convince Steve and Lisa to come back. And your mom, of course."

She leaned back and looked at him as if he'd gone nuts. "What are you talking about?"

"From what I understand, they have pretty nice weddings out there."

Her hand went to her chest. "Excuse me?"

He smiled, loving this. Loving her. "What do you say you make an honest man of me?"

"Get married?" Her voice had gone real high, real soft.

"If you'll have me."

Her eyes closed for a long moment, and when she opened them again, they glistened with tears. "Oh, God, yes."

"Whew," he said. "I was afraid you were going to laugh in my face."

She slugged him on the arm then wrapped her arms around his neck. "Never, never, never. I love you, you twit. I've always loved you."

He pulled back, caressed her face with both hands and looked deep into her blue eyes. "Turns out, I love you, too. And I always will."

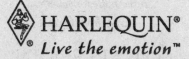

If you enjoyed what you just read,
then we've got an offer you can't resist!

Take 2 bestselling love stories FREE!

Plus get a FREE surprise gift!

Clip this page and mail it to Harlequin Reader Service®

IN U.S.A.	IN CANADA
3010 Walden Ave.	P.O. Box 609
P.O. Box 1867	Fort Erie, Ontario
Buffalo, N.Y. 14240-1867	L2A 5X3

YES! Please send me 2 free Blaze™ novels and my free surprise gift. After receiving them, if I don't wish to receive anymore, I can return the shipping statement marked cancel. If I don't cancel, I will receive 4 brand-new novels each month, before they're available in stores! In the U.S.A., bill me at the bargain price of $3.80 plus 25¢ shipping and handling per book and applicable sales tax, if any*. In Canada, bill me at the bargain price of $4.21 plus 25¢ shipping and handling per book and applicable taxes**. That's the complete price and a savings of at least 10% off the cover prices—what a great deal! I understand that accepting the 2 free books and gift places me under no obligation ever to buy any books. I can always return a shipment and cancel at any time. Even if I never buy another book from Harlequin, the 2 free books and gift are mine to keep forever.

150 HDN DNWD
350 HDN DNWE

Name	(PLEASE PRINT)	
Address	Apt.#	
City	State/Prov.	Zip/Postal Code

* Terms and prices subject to change without notice. Sales tax applicable in N.Y.
** Canadian residents will be charged applicable provincial taxes and GST.
  All orders subject to approval. Offer limited to one per household and not valid to current Blaze™ subscribers.
  ® are registered trademarks of Harlequin Enterprises Limited.

BLZ02-R

HARLEQUIN® *Blaze*™
HARLEQUIN® *Temptation*®

Single in South Beach

Nightlife on the Strip just got a little hotter!

Join author Joanne Rock as she takes you back to Miami Beach and its hottest singles' playground. Club Paradise has staked its claim in the decadent South Beach nightlife and the women in charge are determined to keep the sexy resort on top. So what will they do with the hot men who show up at the club?

GIRL GONE WILD
Harlequin Blaze #135
May 2004

DATE WITH A DIVA
Harlequin Blaze #139
June 2004

HER FINAL FLING
Harlequin Temptation #983
July 2004

Don't miss the continuation of this red-hot series from Joanne Rock!

Look for these books at your favorite retail outlet.

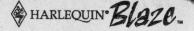
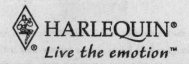